THE CHIMERA'S APPRENTICE

THE CHIMERA'S APPRENTICE

ROSLYN MUIR

PUBLISHED BY RAINSCAPE MEDIA INC.

Publisher's note: This is a work of fiction. Any reference to historical events, real people or real places, are used fictitiously. Names and characters are products of the author's imagination and any resemblance to actual people, living or dead, or business are purely coincidental.

Issued in print and electronic formats

ISBN (paperback)   978-1-7772839-0-2
ISBN (epub)   978-1-7772839-1-9

Library and Archives Canada Cataloguing in Publication information is available on request.

Cover design: Elena Dudina
Cover models: Erika McKitrick & Vaughan Cameron
Book design: KH Formatting

Published by Rainscape Media Inc.
www.roslynmuir.com

Dedicated to all the children in my life, big and small, who continue to inspire me.

Chimera: pronounced ki-mer-a

1. Greek mythology: a fire-breathing she-monster having the heads of a lion, a goat and a dragon

2. an imaginary monster made of bizarre parts

3. an illusion or creation of the mind—an unrealizable dream

Chapter One

There was a soft rustling coming from the box in the centre of my project's display, and I was doing my best to talk over it. I proudly gestured to my lifecycle-of-the-rat poster I had taped to the chalkboard behind me: it was a work of art.

"No one at the time knew it," I continued, "the rats carried fleas infected with the Black Plague—a deadly disease." My fingers began to sweat and stick to the plastic report cover. "As a result, rats have a bad reputation. Two centuries ago, *rattus norvegicus*, the Norwegian or Brown rat, was brought to North America on ships and is now the most common mammal on Earth. However, rats are intelligent creatures that have colonized the world and refuse to go away."

Thump. Thump. Thump. A look of bewilderment crossed Mrs. Whittlestone's face as she watched from her desk. Could she hear it? Her black hair was pulled in a too-tight bun, pen poised to make notes. Tap, tap, tap. Her pen hit the desk and she offered me a kind, get-on-with-it smile.

I wiped my damp hand on my jeans, took a deep breath and kept reading, allowing the emotion in my voice to grow with each word. "Rats spread throughout North America as quickly as its immigrants built houses, farms, and businesses."

Thump. Thump. Thump.

"It's almost like we belonged together, human and rat." It was my favorite sentence. Then the box jumped and there was a snicker from someone at the back of the class. I ignored them both. "Human and rat," I said again, louder.

Mrs. Whittlestone hiccupped.

The box moved again.

My classmates craned their necks to ogle it.

I glanced at my paper but had lost my place on the page.

Thump. Thump. Thump.

"Kyra, what is—" began Mrs. Whittlestone, but it was too late.

Out of the box burst two gigantic, wild grey rats—Norwegian Browns—their long, wormy tails flailing back and forth. I'd worked so hard to capture the two most perfect specimens I could find. Early this morning I baited a cardboard box with some tuna and set it in the alley behind the school. At first all I caught was the neighbourhood tomcat, which snarled and hissed at me. Then I filled the box with more tuna and set it near a garbage can. It worked!

As the rats raced towards the door and a screaming Mrs. Whittlestone, a couple of things became clear. One: I should've used a better box. Two: the rats were memorable—maybe *too* memorable.

"And that's why I'm suspended," I explained to my mom later that day.

"You brought live rats to school? Real rats? Do you know how dangerous that was? They're disgusting!" Mom glanced suspiciously around the living room of our tidy but run-down apartment as if expecting a rat to appear from under the couch. "Where did you find them?"

"You said I should get a hobby."

"I meant painting or knitting," she said.

Knitting, really? How many droopy socks does a person need?

"Why are you so obsessed with these creatures?" she asked. I shrugged. Obsessed? Harsh.

"Then Mrs. Whittlestone slapped the big red panic button on the wall. And Mr. Crenshaw, the principal, rushed in just as she fainted."

"Kyra Murch, what have you done?" Crenshaw had bellowed as he fanned Mrs. Whittlestone's ashen face.

While my frightened classmates screamed and jumped up on their desks, I had to suppress a grin. Those incredible rats had escaped the box all by themselves. Using their sharp teeth, they chewed through the thick cardboard, and when they jumped off the table, they flew through the air like birds. As they scrambled down the hallway to freedom, I wished they'd taken me with them.

Only one person hadn't seemed mad at me—Mrs. Glip, the principal's hundred-year-old office administrator. Rumour had it that she was the one who really ran the school. Earlier, while I sat in Mr. Crenshaw's office awaiting my punishment, she had peered over her heavy green-framed glasses to greet me warmly. Her purple candy floss hair gleamed under the office lights, her possum face bright pink.

"Are you listening to me?" Mom asked.

"Huh?" I blinked.

"Kyra!" Mom's face was the exact same shade of pink as she flicked her mane of black curls over her shoulder. Her sparkling green eyes turned dull grey with anger. "Rats are filthy, disease-ridden vermin."

"No, they're smart. And they have families, and morals and—and they're so cool. This never would've happened if you'd let me have one for a pet!"

"Kyra!" She stood there a moment, her mouth wide as her anger bubbled over. She finally spoke in her stern, you're-in-big-trouble voice, "Clean your room and do your laundry. Just because you're suspended doesn't mean you're on vacation."

The cellphone rang, its siren song calling Mom back to her home office where she did computer accounting. But as she left the living room, she mumbled under her breath, "You're just like your father."

"I am? Good," I blurted.

She turned back to me with a look of horrible disappointment. I felt instantly ashamed. But it was kinda true.

After a few moments of feeling like a super-big jerk, I crept down the hallway towards my room. I paused at her office door, unsure whether it was too late to apologize. I pushed the door open a bit and wrinkled my nose as the Sweet Rose air freshener spray she loved wafted over to me. Mom had the cellphone tucked under her chin and fingers flying across the computer keyboard, working hard to keep it all together. It wasn't easy without Dad around. And now I had disappointed her.

Suspended. Only the bad kids at school got suspended. I bit my lip, suppressing a grin. I never did anything bad. In fact, I went out of my way to stay out of trouble.

I closed my bedroom door softly behind me. My room was a disaster; my rat research was everywhere. Practice posters littered the floor. Research books and note cards covered my bed. Maybe Mom was right—my rat report had become an obsession. I swept everything onto the floor and threw myself onto the bed, mad at the injustice of it all. If my teacher hadn't been so afraid of rats, if the rats hadn't escaped, if the other kids hadn't screamed so loud, I would've aced the project.

Maybe.

The hamster calendar loomed above me on the wall. Glittery stars and big arrows in felt pen pointed to the day I would shine—today—but it had all gone wrong. I just wanted to be good at something. What was wrong with that?

I ran a finger over the glittery stars. Tomorrow was my thirteenth birthday. I used to look forward to birthdays, but today I'd had a nagging feeling that something bad was going to happen. And it did.

Rats.

I turned away from the wall. My eyes landed on the framed family photo on my bedside table. In the photo, Mom, Dad, and I were standing in what looked like a park under a crazy looking tree, a monkey puzzle tree I think it was called. Although I was very small and don't remember getting the photo taken at all, I knew it was special. It was the only picture of us all together.

I don't look like my mom. I don't look like my dad either. I have blue eyes like him and this boring blond hair that I've dyed too many times. It's mostly pink now. Dad used to say I must've stolen my hair from some other baby in the hospital where I was born because no one in the family looked like me. It was one of those things he always joked about as he tucked me into bed at night.

I don't know if I have real memories of Dad or if it's just been Mom talking about him all the time. She used to cry late at night after he left, but I wasn't sure what to say. Dad's been away for a really long time. Years. He used to send me postcards, but he hadn't written or called or come home for a visit in forever. It was like he didn't even exist anymore. Mom once said he was in Iraq or Afghanistan or some faraway place like that, but I'd seen the news on TV. Soldiers came home eventually—dead or alive.

I grabbed Mercy, my stuffed animal from when I was about four. Mercy was a big grey mouse with buttons for eyes and soft, pink, fuzzy ears. She wore a blue checked dress and a white apron. She wasn't a store-bought toy; someone had actually stitched her by hand. The stuffing was crinkly and heavy, and she smelled like chocolate chip cookies. Mercy was the only toy I could never let go of. When I was little, Mercy and I used to have tea parties together. We would sit for hours talking about stuff, planning the fun things we were going to do, the people we were going to be. I didn't talk to her much anymore, but sometimes she was the only friend I had. I pulled her into a tight embrace.

"Oh, Mercy, what am I going to do? I'm so embarrassed. I can never go back to school," I whispered into her velvety cheek. She offered no answers. Why did I have to figure out all this stuff by myself?

I grabbed my laundry basket and trudged down to the basement.

"Your Majesty," nodded Mr. Varve, our building caretaker, as I passed him on the stairs. It was our private joke. I went through an embarrassing princess phase (I wore a tiara all through grade three) and it kind of stuck. I gave him a sullen nod, avoiding eye contact.

If you looked up "weird" in the dictionary you'd find Varve's photo. He always dressed in a crisp white shirt and pants and there was never a dirty spot on his clothes. Ever. His dark brown hair was slicked back with some oil that smelled like almonds, and I could usually smell him before I could see him. Under his breath he sang, "Hunka hunka burning love." He loved some old singer named Elvis. But what was even weirder was the fact that he had been the building manager at every apartment we'd ever lived at. All four of them. Yeah, Varve was odd, but Mom was a bit strange too. Mom was a serial mover.

I'd been to a lot of different schools and never really fit in. I wasn't so good at talking to other kids—what was the point? We'd be leaving soon anyways. Mom said I think too much, that I made up stories in my head all the time and didn't look around me. I really didn't see anything wrong with that.

The laundry room was eerily quiet. It was a small room: washers on one side, dryers on the other, and a gleaming white wall in the back. A creepy feeling overcame me like someone was watching me. I held my breath, threw the clothes in the washer, and shoved the coins in. To heck with the soap. Something went through me—a feeling, a shiver, like I knew I was in danger.

That's when it happened. The craziest, weirdest thing ever.

I dropped the laundry basket and let out a squeak. At the door was a little man, but it wasn't really a man, even though "it" was standing on two legs. He had a thick snout like a dog and long, long whiskers. His black nose was shiny and wet; a limp pink tongue hung out of his panting mouth. Goggles covered a worn leather flight cap, and he wore a too-tight army uniform with mismatched brass buttons about to pop open. A furry little paw with long, sharp black claws held up a smooth, milky-looking stone. Was it a weapon?

"Kyra of Murch, I've come to take you home." And then he laughed, an evil, maniacal laugh like the bad guys in the movies.

"Uh, I'm not Kyra Murch. You have the wrong person," I lied. I was talking to a RAT. A walking, talking rat-man. Impossible. But soooo amazing!

"I'd recognize a Murch anywhere," he sniffed the air, advancing towards me. "I can't believe my luck. You're here! Ha! I've succeeded!"

This wasn't happening. I was talking to a rat. It was real. And I was seriously trapped. He was smaller than me, about the size of a ten-year-old. I could do some moves on him. I'd seen *Karate Kid*. But I wasn't much of a fighter; in fact, I hated seeing people get hurt.

"Are you going to throw that little rock at me, rat face?" I bluffed.

The rat-man was stunned. "Er, this is an ancient weapon. You can't insult the Adularia. There are only two in existence, and the Raturro have protected them for eons. The Adularia is, er, all-powerful." He held the weapon out towards me as if to show me.

"I'm warning you," I stood as tall as I could. "This is your last chance!"

The rat-man's eyes went wide. He was scared of me!

"So shoot me! Get it over with already!" I bellowed, gaining some momentum.

"I-I'm not here to shoot you." He lowered his weapon. "I'm sorry. I didn't mean to scare you. I'm Shale of the Deep Nestling Raturro." He held out one of his paws for me to shake, then changed his mind. "I've come to save you. You're in grave danger."

"Deep what?"

"They're coming for you."

"They?" I asked, curious. "Who? There's more of you?"

But he didn't answer me. He only choked out a tiny squeak. Something on the wall behind me caught his attention.

"It's the m-monster—" he stammered. "Run!"

A flash of blinding light came from behind me. Before I could turn to look, the wall went hot. Like fire. I was sucked against it by some unseen force. Glued to it. I couldn't move. I thought at first that I'd been hit by the rat-man's weapon, but the bright light coming from behind me turned orange and grew hotter.

My right arm tingled and against my will it lifted away from the wall and pointed at the rat-man. BAM! A blue bolt of electricity shot out of the tip of my finger and hit him point-blank on the chest.

"I'm sorry!" I spluttered, worried I'd hurt him. "That wasn't me."

The stone weapon dropped from his paw and rolled under the dryer, and the shocked rat-man rose up in the air suspended by a beam of orange light coming out of the wall.

"Run, Kyra of Murch. Run!" he squealed and shot past me *through* the wall. Really. He went right through the wall behind me. A thick concrete wall. There's no way that could've happened.

Then it was over and whatever held me let go. I fell to the ground, my legs all warm and tingly, my arm aching. When I glanced back at the wall I saw three pairs of red glowing eyes, staring at me. For a moment all I could do was stare back, and then the red lights faded out. They were gone.

I don't remember running up the stairs, but I swear I screamed all the way to our apartment.

I sat on the couch next to Mom, who tried to calm me down. I don't know how Varve knew, but he burst through the door all commando-like wondering what the noise was about.

"The basement—" I started, but my mouth was parched. Mom and Varve stared at me, waiting for me to finish. "A man." I knew they'd think I was crazy if I told them the truth. Or what I thought was the truth because I wasn't really sure. Talking rats don't exist, I told myself. They don't. They don't. They don't.

Varve's usual upbeat personality was gone. He was taller, on alert, and exchanged worried looks with Mom who'd gone very pale.

"It's him," she whispered.

"I'll check, Aerikka," he said to her. "Don't you worry."

After Varve left, we sat there for a very long time, not speaking, Mom hugging me, trying to reassure me. It seemed forever before Varve walked back through the door with the laundry basket in his arms.

"There's no one down there," he said, calmly. Varve and Mom shared a long look that I didn't understand and, though Mom seemed relieved, she pulled me even closer. She let out a troubled sigh. I bet she thought I'd made the whole thing up. But I didn't. It really happened. At least, that's what I kept telling myself.

Chapter Two

"Have you heard from Dad?" I asked, trying to fill the awkward silence. We'd been sitting staring at each other for a long, uncomfortable hour. He would believe me, even if Mom and Varve didn't.

"What?" Mom seemed confused, and she and Varve shared another odd look. "Sweetie, I don't know where he is or how to reach him."

My dad was a rational man, a soldier. He'd help me find an explanation, and I really wanted an explanation for what I saw. It had to be real.

"Maybe you could try."

"I can't. You know that," she replied.

"Don't you think it's strange that you don't hear from him very often? Ever? I don't get it."

Varve cleared his throat; his eye went to the door. Mom wrung her hands, but her voice had a soft tone. "I know it's hard to understand, Kyra, but he's doing important work—"

"You can tell me where he is, Mom. I miss him. I want to see him."

Mom sighed. "I know it's hard, but I honestly don't know where he is."

I didn't believe her. "But how can that be possible? Is he a spy? Is he in jail? Are you divorced?"

Varve shuffled towards the door. "Aerikka, I should get back—"

"No, Kyra. Of course not. You need to realize that sometimes adults have to do something so vital that telling anyone about it can put them in terrible danger."

The door shut with a swoosh; Varve had left. Mom and I stared at each other for a long moment. So she knew Dad was doing something so extreme that she could barely speak about it. Why couldn't I know the secret? I really missed him. Why didn't he come back?

"I'm going to check the mail. Maybe he sent me a birthday card."

"Kyra, wait!" Mom followed me to the kitchen. "He hasn't sent you a card in years."

"Yeah, I noticed." I snapped at her. I grabbed the key off the hook and ran out of the apartment.

The mailbox was empty. No letter, no birthday card. I slammed it shut. Dad had forgotten about me. Again.

After a moment I glanced over at the stairwell that led to the basement. Did I really see that weird rat-man? Maybe it was some kind of prank to pay me back for what happened at school. Maybe some clues were left to prove how it was pulled off.

I swallowed my fear and took the stairs two at a time. Mom had told me not to go back down to the basement without her or Varve along, but I needed to know if I was going crazy, seeing things or if that weirdness really happened.

The laundry room door was shut tight. It took a moment before I was finally brave enough to push the door open and switch on the light. The familiar hum of fluorescent lights started up. I chewed on my lip, unsure if I should venture into the room again, but it looked innocent enough. No trace of anything that had happened. Nothing.

I stepped inside the room and stared at the wall where I'd seen the red eyes. I tried to think of other excuses for what had happened, but it all seemed too real.

The wall still smelled like fresh paint. If electricity had travelled through the wall it would've left a mark, wouldn't it? I bravely placed my hand on it, but it was cold and lifeless. I ran my hand over it searching for a trap door. Nothing. No button, or secret window. Nothing. The strange events played in my head again. I saw the rat-man and the burning red eyes and a chill ran down my spine. That was no prank.

I placed my ear against the cold wall, listening. Again, nothing.

"Kyra of Murch, I've come to take you home," I whispered to the wall, leaning my forehead on it, willing something to happen. "Hey, Rat-man."

Nothing.

I politely knocked on the wall. "Hello? Are you in there? Mr. Rat? Um, Mr., um, from Deep, er, something? Shale?"

No answer.

I kicked it. "Stupid wall."

Disappointed, I leaned my back against the wall and ran my eyes over every inch of the room. I had imagined the entire thing. But the wall felt warm and comforting somehow. A tingling sensation crawled up my back, but it wasn't my fear this time. The wall had grown warmer. And then it happened again. I couldn't move. A growing heat moved through my body, and my brain tingled and sizzled. When I was finally able to turn my head I saw a pair of piercing red eyes, wrinkled around the edges and with long dark pupils.

I pulled away from the force that held me and fell to the floor. When I looked back at the wall, three pairs of red eyes were staring right at me. My chest went tight and I could barely breathe.

One pair of eyes grew larger, surrounded by waves of bright light as a dragon's head formed, the colour of fire. As it came out of the wall, long razor-sharp fangs grew from its mouth and I thought it would eat me. But its gaze flickered towards the second pair of eyes as a shimmering lioness's head materialized. It too floated out from the wall on a long neck to look me over but quickly lost interest. The lion turned to face the dragon as if they were talking a silent, secret language. I was sure they were arguing over who was going to devour me first. I took advantage of the moment and crawled towards the dryers where I cowered like a frightened four-year-old.

The third pair of eyes grew a strange goat's head, with extra long horns and sharp fangs. It had a fiery orange glow. A single body emerged connecting them all, like a drawing made of light. This three-headed monster had iridescent wings, a long tail, clawed front paws, and hooves on its back legs. The light was dazzling but I dared not move my hand to shield my eyes, afraid the monster would pounce. As suddenly it appeared, the monster faded back into the wall and for a moment there was just a dark outline of the creature—like some bizarre graffiti. And the glow of six red eyes.

The laundry room was pretty quiet after that. Except for the desperate sound of my panting, the drips of sweat hitting the floor, and the haunting buzz of the lights. Everything seemed to slow down, but I forced myself back over to the wall.

My trembling hand rested on the cool surface, and I was stunned as warmth flowed into me. I found myself smiling in amazement, no longer afraid. There was something so awe-inspiring about the monster. What was it? Where did it come from?

A soothing female whisper came through the wall. It reminded me of the feeling you get from a hug, and then a word rose up out of the warmth and left my lips. "*Chimera.*"

"Chimera," I whispered to Mercy as I held her tight and tried to figure out what had just happened. I'd snuck past Mom into my room. She'd never guess I'd been back to the basement. As I lay on my bed I could still feel the strange warmth inside of me, although it was fading. I tried to focus on it, hold onto it, but I had no idea how to feel anymore. "Chimera," I whispered again, trying out the new word. "It spoke to me."

Then Mom entered my room and sat next to me on the bed, a small wooden box in her hands. "It's your birthday tomorrow, Kyra. Thirteen. Wow. I've been saving this for you."

"Oh, gee. Thanks, Mom." I held the box unsure what to do. She never gave me presents early. We always had a routine. Cards and presents on the table. Dinner and cake. Dishes cleared. Then I could open the presents.

"Go ahead, open it."

I flipped open the box and pulled out a thick bracelet of tarnished silver. In the centre was a round piece of black stone, rough and scarred with faded wisps of white through it. There was a faded design, a barely visible swirly, snaky creature. The bracelet looked very old, ancient, like it had taken a beating.

"This has been in our family for a long, long time," she continued.

"I thought we didn't have any family." Everyone had died before I was born. I'd never met any grandparents, uncles, aunts, or cousins. Mom never liked to talk about anything from the past. So why did she suddenly act as if it was part of a history we shared?

As I held the bracelet, there was a look of sadness in her eyes like she was giving me something that was precious to her and didn't really want to let it go. It was an odd present. I didn't have any jewelry and wasn't really into it. In fact, I wasn't sure that I wanted it.

"I need you to keep this bracelet on. Don't ever, *ever* take it off. Do you understand?" Mom talked rapidly as she took the bracelet from me and clasped it on my wrist.

"Why?" The bracelet was a family treasure, yet it weighed almost nothing at all. But Mom was instantly assured and let out a big sigh.

"Just promise me." She gave me an intense look, as if everything was riding on my response.

"Um, sure, Mom," I whispered, too tired to object and not yet knowing the weight of those words.

Then she took my hand in hers, "Oh, you're so cold. Are you feeling alright?"

They say we're made up of millions of molecules and atoms, and they're all in a certain order to make us look like people. I felt like my atoms had been rearranged and hadn't yet found a shape. Suddenly exhausted, I lay down on the bed, Mercy cradled in my arms, too tired to change out of my clothes.

"I'm just tired," I told her.

Mom kissed my forehead. "Happy Birthday, Kyra" was the last thing I heard as I dozed off into a deep, deep sleep.

I was so groggy the next morning that I knocked over the family photo, cracking the glass frame. When I set it back on the table, it seemed to glow in the darkened room. I could've sworn the colour had changed too. Once dull and ordinary, now it was brighter: the sun sparkled on Mom's hair and Dad stood like an athlete, all tanned and full of glory. We seemed so happy together against the lush green trees. Why couldn't we be like that now?

I got up and changed into fresh clothes, determined to get to school before everyone else. I was suspended, but it wasn't going to stop me from investigating the chimera. I grabbed the photo out of the broken frame and tucked it into my shirt pocket, leaving before Mom was even awake. I felt bad not saying goodbye to her, but I was on a mission and I didn't want her to stop me.

Suddenly I was standing on the street, facing the morning and doubting myself. Did all that really happen? Did I really see a three-headed monster made of light?

I trudged along the sidewalk to the end of the street and ducked down a back alley. The closer I got to school, the older the buildings in the alley appeared. The tarred street turned into cobblestones. I felt a warm sensation on my wrist and pulled back my jacket to look at the bracelet. I touched the dark stone.

Onyx. Microcrystalline quartz.

"Huh?" How did I know that?

The old cobblestones beneath my feet seemed to vibrate.

Granite. Igneous rock formed by magma. Key components: silica, quartz, feldspar, and mica.

"What?"

I jumped off the cobblestones to a strip of concrete that ran along the side of a brick building. The ingredients of the concrete floated into my head: *sand, limestone, calcium, silicon, aluminum.* The information just appeared in my head like some random database. Where did that come from?

"Kyraaa."

"Huh?" I jumped, but there wasn't anyone else in the alley with me.

"Kyraaa," the eerie voice continued.

"Who's there?" My voice echoed down the empty alley, but no one answered. Maybe that rat-man was back. The sound of rustling paper came from behind a dumpster, and then a foot-long grey rat poked its nose out at me. It crept out of the shadows dragging its long, pink tail like a fat worm.

"What do you want? Leave me alone." The rat stared at me a moment and scurried back behind the dumpster. A man carrying some trash had stopped and was staring at me like I was crazy, so I ran out of the alley as fast as I could.

When I got to school I snuck down a quiet side hallway and headed straight for the library, knowing only a few early risers would be there catching up on homework. I had to find out what that monster was, and the library always had the answer. It was the first place I hung out when I started a new school. The only place I felt welcome. And this school library was so great I didn't even need to go to the public library. They had it all.

I stopped in front of one of the catalogue computers and punched in the word I had heard. It took me a few tries before I got the spelling right: chimera.

I could've used Mom's computer, but I didn't want her to discover my search. Besides, I loved real books in real libraries. As I walked down a long aisle, I ran my hand over the books. I used to play a game where I'd close my eyes and walk down the aisle. Then I'd randomly stop and tug a book off the shelf, unseen—no matter what the title was I'd make myself read it. Best game ever!

I found what I was looking for—a big glossy tome on mythology and hefted it to a nearby table. I scanned through the book and there it was—the chimera.

"It's a creature from Greek mythology. Pronounced ki-mer-a," I whispered, my finger resting on a picture of an ancient stone engraving. "It has the heads of a dragon, lion, and goat, a female creature…can breathe fire…is very protective. An omen of storms, shipwrecks, and disasters." I stopped. The chimera was a myth—made up—but it had seemed so real. No, it *was* real.

The bracelet was suddenly hot and heavy like it was made of lead, and an image flickered in my head: a huge, evil-looking rat-man with big, yellowed fangs and a torn ear. He laughed even more maniacally than the rat-man in the laundry room. He was in our living room! Two other huge rat-men held Mom by the arms. "Where is it?" the evil one asked and hit her across the face leaving claw marks that bled.

I shrieked.

The entire library jumped. The diminutive librarian gave me a suspicious glare. "Kyra Murch. Aren't you suspended?"

I sprinted the twelve blocks home. I hoped it was just my imagination, but I had a sinking feeling in my heart that I had seen something real. I was shaking so badly I could barely get my key in the front door. Dashing up the stairs, I reached our apartment out of breath. The door wasn't shut properly and deep scratches gouged the cheap wood frame. Afraid of what I might find, I slowly pushed the door open.

The entire apartment had been trashed. Tables. Lamps. Chairs. Everything we owned was toppled over, destroyed. Even the pillows on the couch were ripped open, their fluffy white contents strewn about the floor. I picked up a pillow ripped by large claw marks.

"Mom?" My voice faltered, but I knew she was gone. I ran from room to room, but she was nowhere to be found.

My bedroom was the worst hit. Whoever, whatever, had been here had even ripped Mercy to shreds. I picked her up off the floor. Her head hung off her body and one of the little white buttons that used to be her eye hung from a long thread. My hand trembled, and the button came loose in my hand. I slipped the pearly button into my jeans pocket. Then I couldn't stop the tears.

"Mom?" I whispered and pulled the remnants of Mercy close to my chest.

A noise came from the living room. Someone was in the apartment. Was it the rat-man? I shut my eyes tightly not wanting to know, not wanting to see, but when my bedroom door swung open I couldn't help myself. I had to look. Before me stood a man wearing green army fatigues. He was tall and daunting, his white hair oddly disheveled. It took me a moment to recognize him.

"Dad?" I stammered. It couldn't be.

His face, once handsome in my photograph, was disfigured on one side from a wound that left his skin bubbled and pocked. His once brown hair was brilliant white, his skin pale. He was much older than I remembered.

"Kyra! Thank goodness you're safe!"

I ran into his arms and he hugged me tight. "Daddy!" Hot tears burned my eyes.

"Everything's going to be okay," he said.

"I thought you were dead." I peered up at him. "Where's Mom?" A pained look came over his face. More footsteps in the living room, and suddenly Varve was in the doorway. Instead of his shiny white caretaker's uniform, he too was dressed in army fatigues and had an intense look in his eyes.

"We must go," said Dad.

"What about Mom? Where is she?"

BLEEP. Varve pulled out a strange electronic device, a GPS-type thing with a screen flashing with little green lights. "They're within the perimeter."

"If we don't go now, we'll never save your mother," said Dad.

"Tell me where she is," I said.

"We won't make it," urged Varve, worried.

Dad put his hands on my shoulders. "You have to trust me, Kyra, or we're all dead."

Dead? Now I was really afraid. Was everything that Shale said coming true? Was he really trying to help me?

With Varve in front, we hustled down the stairwell and into the basement. Although I barely had time to think, I wasn't surprised when Dad led me into the laundry room. Varve stood guard at the door and pulled a weapon out from beneath his jacket, ready for an assault.

Dad turned to Varve. "Don't leave any evidence." He ushered me towards the wall and it burst into light. The chimera! It didn't snake out of the wall this time, just glowed like it was a brilliant window; one moment it was solid, then it was translucent. It held me in its sights. I couldn't move, couldn't even tremble in fear.

"Hold your breath, Kyra," said Dad.

"Why?"

"We're going to the other side." He raised his voice as if to shout over a noise only he could hear.

I pulled back from him, tried to struggle away, but there was nowhere to go. "No, I want to find Mom. Where is she?" I cried.

"They're here," shouted Varve.

Dad threw his arms around me and lifted me off the ground. "Hold your breath," he commanded.

I filled my lungs and wondered if I should hold my nose like when jumping into the deep end of a swimming pool. Eyes tightly shut, we moved through the wall as if it were only light. I felt that feeling again—the warmth—and then I was inside of something so wonderful, I didn't want to let go.

CHAPTER THREE

I woke up on a cold stone floor, scared of what I might find. Dad's arms were around me, gently shaking me to life. It had only taken a few seconds to move through the wall, but it felt like being sucked up the nozzle of a vacuum cleaner. What just happened? We had walked through a wall made of concrete. How was that even possible? Even more crazy, we had travelled through a monster made of light.

Granite. Elements of the stone popped unwelcome into my head. The room was skillfully carved out of rock. I somehow knew I was below ground in the middle of a mountain.

With Dad's help I stood up; my head swam and ached. Coming through the chimera didn't seem to bother him.

"Where's Mom?" I asked, surprised that I could even summon up my voice. "Is she dead?"

"Are you okay?"

"Where is she?"

"No, she's not dead, Kyra. She's too valuable," he sighed.

"What do you mean?" I said.

"She's been taken by the rebel Raturro."

"I don't understand. Why would someone take Mom?"

"The Raturro are a violent race of mutant rats. They walk and talk like humans, but they're still animals. The rebel faction have killed thousands of our people and almost destroyed the city."

"Rats. I saw one and then it—" I glanced around at the chimera which now sat on the wall like some huge engraved coat of arms. Its eyes weren't bright red anymore; the light was out.

"Yes, the chimera saved you. She told me. When Murch City was overthrown by the rebel Raturro," he continued. "I led our people here, to the Armory. We had to retreat, build up our weapons, but we're almost ready for the final assault."

"*Murch* City?"

"I thought you'd both be safe far away from here. I don't know how they found you. They must've opened a portal somehow. I'm sure the rebels are holding her in the Reach." He led me to the window, and I couldn't believe my eyes. Below us in the hollowed-out cavern was a huge military base. There were weapons and tanks and soldiers running about, but we were hundreds of feet above it in our own little quiet grey cocoon.

"You're fighting a war? Where are we?" I stammered. I just couldn't believe he was right in front of me, after so many years.

"You're safe here and that's all that matters. All these people are under my command and will protect you. But the less you know about where we are and our plans, the better," he said.

Why was he keeping the truth from me? All adults were the same. Secrets and lies.

"I'll bring your mother back. Soon. Don't you worry about that, Kyra. Majellan will pay for it. He'll pay dearly."

"Who's Majellan?" The look on Dad's face said that it was someone he hated.

"No one you should worry about," he covered.

I peered down again at all the military equipment and soldiers he had at his disposal. If he was the leader, couldn't he just order them to find Mom?

"But Dad—Ow! My head!" My brain went fuzzy, like I was swimming through the wall again.

"It's a reaction to coming through the stone," he said. "The chimera is an ancient device. A portal that helps us travel through stone…through worlds. It's difficult to explain…." His voice faded in and out. There was a pressure and a tingling sensation in my head. I turned back to the wall and faced the chimera as if it had called to me. Just looking at it made me feel comforted and fearful at the same time. I wanted to touch it, discover its secrets, know its inner workings.

"What is that thing?" I pulled away from Dad and went towards the monster. When I finally got to the wall, I hesitated, not sure if I should disturb its sleep. But as I reached out and placed my hand on it—the chimera exploded into light.

"Ahhhh," Dad wailed. He slumped against the window, his head in his hands; he looked so small, rumpled, like a child. He quickly regained his composure and glanced past me to the chimera, suddenly awake and glowing brightly like a giant neon sign. Dad ran to it, eyes darting back and forth, arms up, grasping at air. Then an odd look came over him.

"No, no, this can't be." He concentrated hard, "Chimera, answer me."

Panic washed over him.

I didn't know what his question had been, but he seemed alarmed, worried, devastated even. His jaw dropped and he slowly turned to me, in shock. He grabbed my arm and pulled up my shirtsleeve.

"No, she didn't—"

When he saw the bracelet on my arm his look of anger and disappointment went right through me. "Mom gave it to me for my birthday," I whispered.

"What was she thinking? I warned her not to give you the bracelet. Chimera!" He stormed over to the chimera once more. It shimmered in defiance. "Chimera, answer me! That's an order." No response. "This is a mistake. No, it can't be…."

"What's happening?" I asked. Then I heard it. At first it was a soft, comforting, female voice, "*Welcome to the land of Antiica, Kyraaa,*" then the words buzzed and echoed painfully in my head.

"Did that thing just talk to me?"

"*Yes,*" it replied, three voices in unison. It was the voice I'd heard in the alley.

"What's she saying to you?" Dad demanded, but the tingling in my head went red hot and I fell to my knees, dizzy, nauseated by it all.

He ranted at the chimera, "You know she's not ready. This should never have happened. She's too young to rule— or fight a war!" He was panicking now, pacing.

The heat subsided. How could that thing invade my thoughts?

"Where are we? Where's Antiica?" I stuttered, still on my knees. I needed to know.

Dad's face was sunken, hollow, and defeated. "It's your home, Kyra. Antiica is our home. You're not on Earth anymore."

I stared at him in disbelief.

"*The General is ready to come through the portal. Shall I bring him through?*" The voice screamed in my head.

"Ow!" I grabbed my head again. "The General is ready. Who's that?"

Dad came to attention, a soldier once more. "Varve."

"*There's a complication. Can I act on behalf of Antiica and solve the problem?*" It said. She said. The words were suddenly soothing.

"What did she say?" he asked, his expression worried.

"A complication," I replied, unsure.

"Kyra, I know all of this must seem unreal. It's hard to explain why, but the bracelet connects you to the chimera. She will be your constant companion, your familiar, just as she has been mine for so many years." He lifted his sleeve and revealed a bracelet with the same ornate markings, but a different stone. *Jade.* It was a faded speckled green, the colour of fir trees, battered and dull. "When a bracelet is given to an heir to the throne, the family title is automatically bestowed. The chimera becomes part of you."

"Part of me?"

"Your arrival in Antiica has activated the chimera's bonding response. You have the bracelet, and she believes you have come here to rule. Since you're the heir to the throne, she has an historic duty—"

"Wait. Heir? What throne are you talking about?" I started laughing. I couldn't help it. It sounded so ridiculous. Seeing my dad again was all I've wanted for years, and now it was just a weird dream. He was like a stranger in a fairy tale come to life.

He slowly removed the bracelet from his wrist and held it out like a treasure. Instinctively I reached for it but he pulled it away. "You can never, ever wear both bracelets at once. Do you understand?" He slipped the bracelet into his jacket pocket.

"So your bracelet doesn't work anymore? I don't get any of this."

"You're now the only one who can command the chimera. Kyra, you're of an ancient, royal lineage. You must accept the responsibility. There is no other choice."

He was serious. I was on a different world. Heir to a throne. Impossible. I felt a growing anger inside of me. I'd been kept in the dark for so long.

We both faced the chimera. Her red eyes were dull and lifeless. I clutched the bracelet and could feel the stone beneath my hand. How could such a small thing have such power? I wanted to be back in my bedroom. I wanted our crappy apartment building, but most of all I wanted Mom.

"Kyra, we'll find a way to make this work," Dad said. He leaned down and reached for me, took me in his arms. Even though I was confused and hurt, all the loss and tears I'd been holding inside poured out.

"Daddy," I cried. "I missed you so much."

We held onto each other and his rough, callused hand stroked my hair. One time when I was really little I'd fallen down some stairs and bumped my head. It bled and I wailed in fear. I remembered how good it felt when he scooped me up in his arms and held me tight. Just like then, all my fears melted away, and I tried to hold on to him for as long as I could. I pressed my face into his khaki jacket. It would be okay.

But a feeling of dread travelled through me, and I pulled away. An image popped into my head.

"Varve's hurt," I blurted as I fell to my knees. Fire burned through me as the chimera exploded to life, a lightning bolt of pain in my head. Varve jumped through the wall and crumpled down to the floor.

Dad ran to him, saw that he was still conscious. "Stay with him. I'll get a medic," he said and ran out of the room.

"Kyra," Varve's breathy voice echoed through the cavern. Still blinded by the pain, I crawled to his side and took his outstretched hand. Dark blood soaked through Varve's army jacket, and he winced as a wave of pain went through him. "Tell your mother I'm sorry I let her down. I left my post... tell her I—" he said with all his strength. Then Varve's eyes closed, and he heaved a breathy sigh.

"Varve? Varve!" I shook him. Was he dead? I touched his face and felt the shallow, warm breath from his nostrils. He was still alive, but barely. I took his hand and it seemed like forever until a team of medics burst into the room, stretchers in hand, and Dad followed behind them. The medics set to work, lifting Varve onto the stretcher all the while checking his pulse and opening his bloodied jacket. One medic pressed a clean bandage onto Varve's wound and another placed an oxygen mask over his face.

Dad wrapped his arm around me, lifted me onto another stretcher. "The pain will subside," he said. "It's an unfortunate side effect of bonding with the chimera."

"What if I don't want to?" I whispered, but he didn't answer me. He nodded to the medics, and as they whisked me away I glanced back at the chimera. Neither of us had asked to be connected, and I had no idea what to expect.

But I remembered how Shale had called her a "monster," how he'd been so terrified of her. I felt that fear. But the chimera just napped on the wall, her earlier brilliance faded, oblivious to the chaos inside me.

Chapter Four

Folds of grey curtains surrounded me. I sat on the edge of a gurney as a young doctor with large red eyeglasses shone a light in my eyes.

"Headache?" she asked.

"Yes," I said, rubbing my forehead. "Here. And here." I moved my hand to my temple.

"It should pass soon. Get plenty of rest." She handed me a small glass vial of yellow oil. "Rub this on your forehead and the back of your neck. It's a plant extract and blocks the pain." She opened the grey curtain and revealed a soldier in mismatched army fatigues. She saluted, stared right at me. She was about the same age as me, her long red hair tied up in a tight bun. Her look was serious, severe. I didn't know if I was supposed to salute back so I lamely lifted my hand.

"Follow me," she ordered and crisply turned.

I eased myself off the gurney, still clasping the unopened vial. The world teetered for a moment. I turned back to the doctor. "Wait. Varve, is he—"

"He's stable but his condition is critical," she replied.

"Can I see him?" She shook her head no.

The Armory was immense. The soldier led me through a maze of hallways lit by strings of lights dangling from the rough-hewed ceiling. The complex was a series of natural caves and rock formations that had been fortified with concrete. I ran my hand along the wall and I could sense it right away: *igneous rock*. I'd never even used the word '*igneous*' before, but now I knew what it meant—volcanic rock. I tried to remember when this first started happening to me. It must have been when Mom gave me the bracelet. I fingered the cold, black onyx on my wrist. I didn't know why I needed all the knowledge about stones and rocks.

I glanced through a window overlooking the big cavern with all the tanks. Soldiers scurried about, loading tanks and trucks with ammunition and supplies. Ramps led out towards large tunnels, big enough for the tanks to fit through, and towards smaller tunnels that soldiers came and went by. Then I saw him. Dad was still in his green army uniform looking every bit the boss, and soldiers stood at attention when he walked by. My head still pounding, I ditched the soldier and ran back along the hallway where I found a tunnel going downwards.

The soldiers were a green blur; some were the same age as me, maybe even younger. There was an equal number of males and females, all sizes and races, just like on Earth. We were on another world, but everyone looked human. They pointed at me openly like they recognized me. I darted between rows of towering tanks, trying to keep my bearings, trying to avoid the stares. I passed a line of dusty open-top jeeps—they were definitely from Earth. I couldn't be on another world.

I came to a hallway of glass-enclosed caverns that were being used as offices. No signs or numbers were on any of the doors. Dad stood at the head of a long table, meeting with a row of grey-haired, elderly men and women dressed in crisp light-coloured uniforms. He finally glanced up and caught me staring into the office. He half-smiled. The map that was projected on the wall vanished. With a nod from Dad, all the grey-haired people got up and left the room. Dad held the door open and I went in.

"Kyra, I need you to stay upstairs while I get all this sorted out," he said.

"Get what sorted out?" I asked.

"I need to find somewhere safe for you to stay until this war is won," he replied.

"But I don't want to go anywhere. I want to stay here with you. Have you found Mom yet?"

"That's not going to be possible. Without the bracelet, I have no way to find her."

"What? I don't understand." The creeping realization that it was all my fault came into my mind. If I had told Mom what I'd seen in the laundry room, maybe she'd be okay.

"I can't send the army out yet until I verify where she is. If I still had the chimera—" He looked pained. "There's just too much to tell you. I can't do it all right now. There's so much at stake."

"I didn't ask for the bracelet. She gave it to me."

"I know," he said.

"But I can help you, can't I?"

He glanced at me. "You're only a child, Kyra. You can't help in a time like this."

"I'm not a kid anymore. It's my birthday today. I'm thirteen! I can do things; you just need to tell me how it works." I raised my voice and flashed the bracelet at him. I had his attention. "Why are those rat-men trying to kill me?

Why do they want Mom? Why didn't you ever come home?" My face flushed red and my palms began to sweat.

"Sit, Kyra." He pulled a chair out from the table and beckoned me. I had no choice; he was my Dad after all.

After I threw myself down in the chair, he took my hands in his. "You were born here on Antiica. When the unrest started and the rebel Raturro started to attack, I took you and your mother to safety on Earth. For the last five years, I've fought a war with the Raturro—the rat-men—trying to win back our homeland. I've used the portal to bring supplies from Earth. I've lost many good men and women in the fight, but they're all dedicated to winning this war." He gestured towards the glass door and we both looked out at the serious faces of the soldiers and workers. They were readying the tanks for a battle. "Every last one of them will protect you, Kyra. You have nothing to fear." He was serious.

"Am I an alien?"

Dad grinned. "Of course not. We're humans. We came from Earth millennia ago."

"And the chimera?" I whispered, trying to seem brave, but I was overwhelmed.

With this, he sighed heavily. "The chimera is a sentient being that came here from Earth with our ancestors. She will obey you and protect you for as long as you wear that bracelet."

"But she helped me before I even wore the bracelet."

"I sent her to you, Kyra. She has an eye on both worlds, or did." He paced to the glass door. "It takes a lot of training to use the chimera properly, but I can't afford the months it takes to show you. Years, actually. In fact, under normal circumstances you would become the chimera's apprentice and I would train you in her use. But you've come at the worst time—"

"So I'm just supposed to sit around and wait for you to finish your stupid war? You don't care about what happens to Mom. I saw him. That rat-man. He slashed her face. He hurt her. She needs us!"

"What?" Dad reacted in surprise. "What do you mean you *saw* him?"

"In my head."

He was puzzled. "That's impossible."

"Well, it happened." But I could see he didn't believe me.

The female soldier I ditched came to the door and stood at attention. Dad glanced over and nodded at her.

"A room has been assigned to you, and the sergeant will show you the way," he said curtly, then turned to the door and paused, "Oh, and happy birthday, Kyra. I'm sorry I missed it, missed so many." He put his hand on my shoulder. "I'll work on a plan to find Mom, don't worry." He opened the door and I was dismissed like one of his soldiers. Sure, he apologized, but that didn't make me feel any better. Now he was sending me away and my stomach felt like a pit that could never be filled.

I really wanted out of there and quickly followed the soldier out. When I glanced back at him, he had sat down at his desk and buried his head in his hands.

Her name was Sergeant Talia something or other. I didn't catch her last name. I was just too amazed at the Sergeant part. She was so serious and confident. I swear she never blinked once. I could never imagine being like that, not in a million years, but maybe war does that to you, makes you grow up fast.

My new room was a single bedroom with a camp cot, a lamp, and a wooden chair. Nothing much else. The grey blanket and sheets matched the rock out of which the room was carved. Sergeant Talia clicked her heels together, saluted, and left the room.

A clean set of army fatigues sat on the bed, matching green pants and shirt. Was I supposed to put them on? I shoved them under the cot and sat on the hard bed. I couldn't imagine living at the Armory without Mom, never mind wearing a uniform. I missed our crappy apartment building, Varve, and Mercy. I missed school. I even missed Principal Crenshaw and Mrs. Glip. Mrs. Whittlestone not so much.

All that had happened in the past couple of days weighed heavily on me. I was overwhelmed by it all. I was on another *planet*. Another world. Even just thinking it sounded weird. How was I going to get home?

When I woke up, I had no idea how long I'd been sleeping. Sergeant Talia was waiting for me when I ventured out of my room.

"Are you guarding me?" I asked.

"Affirmative," she said.

"Are you going to be with me all the time?"

"Affirmative," she replied without looking at me.

I looked around, unsure what to do. She was going to follow me everywhere. I was starting to feel like a prisoner.

"I've been instructed to take you to the Mess," she said.

"Mess?"

The Mess Hall was the cafeteria, a large room full of long metal tables and wooden benches. The place was mostly empty. Sergeant Talia escorted me to the food counter where all the staff saluted me like I was important, but I was embarrassed at the attention.

"Could you get them to stop doing that?" I asked Sergeant Talia.

"At ease," she instructed the cooking staff.

The wiry cook filled a plate with three pale white meat patties, some mashed orange stuff, and green peas—the only thing I recognized. Sergeant Talia stood above me as I sat at a lone table in the corner. "Uh, at ease?" I said to her, feeling like she watched my every move. "Why don't you grab a drink or something?" She hesitated, then walked off to the beverage table and helped herself to a mug of water. The food tasted pretty good, but I was starving. I could've eaten an old shoe.

A few tables away sat some girls and boys my age dressed as soldiers. They whispered to each other and every so often one of them stared over at me. Halfway through my meal, I couldn't take it anymore, couldn't take being watched and talked about, couldn't take the fact Dad was ignoring me again. I pushed the plate away and got up from the table. Sergeant Talia was quickly at my side.

"I really need to see Dad."

Out on the concourse, as Sergeant Talia called it, we wove in and out of the rows of tanks and trucks. Some were being fixed, their guts spilled on the floor. Some soldiers were cleaning and rebuilding their guns. We walked around the greasy parts and soldiers rapt in their work. The whispers followed us right to Dad's office. I watched him a moment as he leant over his desk, a pencil tucked behind his ear, his face still unshaven. He seemed sad and worn out.

But Dad's face lit up when he finally noticed me. "Kyra, you should be resting."

I threw my arms around him and hugged him tight for as long as I could.

"I know it's a big adjustment being here. You've grown. Some days I thought I'd never see you again." He peeled my arms off him and looked me over. "Yes, you look like your mom now, except for the stolen hair." He remembered our old joke, then winced. "So, pink hair? Is that popular on Earth now?"

Ignoring his question, I got to the point. "When are you going to get her back?"

He hesitated, sat back on his desk. "We're almost ready for the big invasion, to take Murch City back. If we go too soon, we may not be as strong as we could be."

"Couldn't you send in a SWAT team or something?"

"You've been watching too much Earth TV, Kyra. I'm afraid we can't do anything like that. The Raturro are fast and strong. You can never underestimate the enemy. We have spies in Murch City, and I'm waiting for communications so we can pick the optimal strike time. It's all very sensitive."

We stared awkwardly at each other a moment. "But there is something you can help with," he said, eyeing his old watch with the cracked face. "It's just about time." And then he led me out the door.

We went back upstairs to the same level where we had first arrived. When I realized we were going to see the chimera I stopped. "The chimera can find her, can't she?"

Dad turned to me, "Hm?"

"Are we going to find Mom?" I couldn't stop thinking about her. She was some place awful. Hurt. I could feel it.

"Uh, no, not exactly. I need you to open a portal to Earth."

"What?" He mistook my startled look for fear.

"She won't hurt you. The chimera serves you."

"But you said I was too young to use it."

"I was angry. I'm sorry. It was just so unexpected—the sudden disconnection." He looked saddened.

The hairs on my neck rose as we got closer. I wasn't sure what I should feel about this strange monster that could invade my mind. When we arrived in the cavern, the chimera was still sleeping on the wall. Her outline was etched in thick black lines with no hint of the light she held.

Dad stared intently at the chimera, but he could no longer talk to it. He turned to me, took my hand, and spoke softly. "Kyra, I know that contact with the chimera causes pain, but it won't always be that way. I need you to call her and open a portal."

"Can't you take the bracelet?" I tried to remove it, but he stopped me.

"No, it's too late for that. We can't go back. You're the only one the chimera will speak with now."

"I don't want to speak to it. Her."

"She's our only hope."

"What do you mean?"

"The chimera allows us to travel to different parts of Antiica. And you were right, she could help us find Mom."

I stared at the chimera. I didn't understand it, but I knew he was right.

He took me by the shoulders and stood me in front of the chimera. "Once we know where she is, once we have a plan of attack, we will find her. Now, relax your mind."

"But—" I turned away from the chimera, resisting it. I could tell by the grim look on his face that I needed to do it, so I reluctantly closed my eyes and hoped for the best. After a minute of deep breathing, Dad took my hand again.

"Conjure a picture of the chimera in your head. You can will her to come to you, to do your bidding, to help you. But it's going to take quite some time to master it."

"I can do it. I want to learn." I took a big deep breath, curious to see what would happen. If this could help me find Mom, then I was willing to try. In my mind, the chimera came to life. She was bright and big, and there was a noise that I couldn't decipher. I opened my eyes to find the chimera's brilliance shining in front of me. Then the pain came.

And the same vision: Mom in the grips of the evil rat-man. The rat-man slashing her face.

"No!" I cried.

The chimera dulled on the wall.

"Concentrate!" said Dad. "Keep the picture of the chimera in your head, and tell it 'Earth Portal.'"

"But the visions—Mom!"

"Shut them out!"

"She's hurt." I was so worried about her. There had to be a way I could help her.

"Focus!" commanded Dad.

I closed my eyes and concentrated as best I could through the terrible pain in my head and the ache in my heart. I swallowed it down and pushed ahead.

Chimera, I called in my mind. *Chimera, Earth Portal!* Without even opening my eyes, I could see the chimera light up the room. It was terrifying and exciting and just for a moment I felt that warmth again.

"Okay, you can stop now," said Dad, and the room went dark.

I slumped into his arms. I didn't want to cry. Didn't want to let him know how much it hurt. If I couldn't be brave, at least I could pretend to be.

When I finally opened my eyes, Mrs. Glip was standing in front of me. "Your Majesty." She curtsied.

"Mrs. Glip?" I was so relieved to see her. I rushed into her outstretched arms and accepted her warm hug.

"That'll be all, Mrs. Glip. I'll see you and the others in the briefing room," said Dad, impatient.

Mrs. Glip smiled her warm possum smile at me. Then she gave Dad a crisp salute and left the room, followed by a small group of familiar people from back on Earth.

"They've been watching out for you, Kyra." He squeezed my arm, and I felt comforted being so close to him. But then I had a dark thought. Had he sent all these people to spy on me? All these soldiers who saluted him? Everyone knew the truth except me. I longed to go back home and forget about Antiica. I didn't know him at all.

"Kyra, you're very strong," he said proudly. "Even I couldn't hold a portal open for that long on my first try."

"Really?"

He nodded, and I beamed. I'd done something right.

"When I was the chimera's apprentice I wasn't even allowed to go through the portal until I had mastered communicating with her. And I was a lazy student, not like you." His strong arm around me, Dad led me back to my room.

"When can we do that again? The chimera. I should practice. I can do it."

"You should rest now. Later, we'll have dinner and figure out what to do with you." He smiled and ruffled my hair, the way he used to when I was little.

"Ow!"

"Oh, sorry, Kyra. I forgot," he said.

"It's okay. The pain's not that bad," I lied, rubbing my temple. "Dad, do you really think Mom's okay?"

He sighed deeply. "Yes, she's strong. Just like you." I could tell he was troubled, worried, but before I could press him, he abruptly left.

Weary from my contact with the chimera, I lay down on the bed and examined the bracelet on my wrist. It was strange that something so small could connect me with something so big and powerful. I examined the dark stone and wondered how the connection with the chimera worked. What sort of magic did the bracelet have? Did magic really exist or just on Antiica? All I had were a growing list of questions with no answers. With this thought, I dozed off to sleep.

Soon, the vision I had of Mom replayed in my head and I noticed new details. She was panicked but she was also furious, pointing her finger at the vicious Raturro. This time I heard her shout out a name I'd heard before: "Majellan!"

My arms were tightly wound around the pillow when I woke up, covered in sweat. "Majellan?"

CHAPTER FIVE

Dinner was in Dad's quarters, way bigger than the shoebox room I had been given. In addition to his bedroom, he had a sitting room, dining table, and another small office area. There were lots of books and a few photos of Mom and me. Dad saw me glancing around. "I'm working on finding you a bigger room, Kyra. It's just—"

"Not a good time, I know," I said. "Who's Majellan?"

"What?"

"The evil Raturro who took Mom? Why won't you tell me about him?"

Dad was disturbed by my questions, stared blankly at me.

"Dad?"

"Tell me about the visions."

"It's just one vision playing over and over in my head. It's really annoying. What did you do when you had them?"

"I never had them, Kyra. You're sure it's not a dream—"

"I. Saw. It. There was a Raturro in the laundry room then a Raturro in the living room." I spelled it out like he was five.

"Kyra, that condescending attitude—"

Just then there was a knock at the door and a soldier brought our dinner in on a cart. Dad seemed relieved for the distraction. The food looked way better than the stuff in the Mess Hall. The soldier set the plates down, saluted us both and left the room. I was never going to be comfortable with the saluting thing.

I waited for Dad to continue on about my bad attitude but he changed the subject. "So, I've come up with an idea for your stay. I thought you could do basic training with the new recruits. You'll learn how to shoot and fight, in case you encounter the enemy. Everyone in Antiica does basic training, except the Raturro, of course. Even your mother did it. She's a pretty good shot," he said as he tackled a wild salad with deep red leaves.

"Are you kidding?"

"No, she even won an award—"

"That's not what I meant. I don't want to be a soldier. I can't fight. I don't even want to." I furrowed my brow, pushed my plate away.

"Kyra, we're living in a time of war. The more skills you have, the better."

"I won't fight. Ever!" I jumped up from the table. "You didn't answer my question!"

"What question?"

"Majellan. Who is he and why did he take Mom?"

"There's always going to be—" he hesitated, searching for the right word. "Hostages."

"Hostages? So you can pay Majellan money and he'll let her go?"

"Money, no. It's much more complicated than that."

"What does Majellan want? Can't you just give it to him?"

Dad grimaced. "Let's just eat dinner and try to catch up."

"Catch up? My whole world is gone." Tears burned in my eyes. He didn't understand. I turned and ran out of the room.

"Kyra, wait—"

But he didn't follow me.

Sergeant Talia wasn't at her post, so I paced the halls trying to understand what was going on, determined not to cry. What was Dad thinking? He knew Mom was a hostage but he wouldn't negotiate with Majellan?

I heard the clump-clump of approaching army boots so I ducked down a dark hallway. It veered to the left and I followed the tunnel down, down, down. It got darker and darker, and soon I was at the bottom, deep in the bowels of the Armory. I was alone. Glad for the quiet, I leaned against the wall for a moment feeling the newness of the stone. The un-Earthiness of it all. It was so strange to be on another world and be able to feel it in my bones.

And then I heard it. A soft whimper. Curious, I followed the sound.

The small caverns that led off the main hallway were cells for prisoners. Each had heavy metal bars sunk into a concrete base. I was surprised that the area was unguarded, but the cells were empty so I figured they didn't really need guarding.

The whimper was louder now, more like a cry. I followed the sound to its source. In the corner of the very last cell, a large mass of fur heaved and sobbed. A long nose poked out and two beady little eyes opened up. The nose sniffed the air and the thing began to slowly crawl towards me. It had dark grey fur and its legs and arms were thick, muscular—human-like. It reached out a long paw with bloodied stubs; the sharp claws had been pulled out. I winced and backed away.

"Kyra of Murch," it moaned, and I stopped in my tracks. I recognized that voice.

"Mr. Raturro?"

Crawling up against the bars, he didn't look so dangerous anymore. He'd been beaten and tortured since our meeting in the laundry room. His eyes were swollen, teary, and his fur was singed on the side of his head. His uniform was in rags.

"You remember me?" he said, relieved. "My apologies if I frightened you. A terrible business, this war."

"What happened to you?"

"We only had one chance to find you, and I failed in my duty. I was supposed to rescue you before Majellan could find you. He's the leader of the rebel Raturro, once a hero to all. But not so much anymore." He shook his head. "Come closer, child. I'm Shale of the Deep Nestling Raturro."

I inched closer. "Tell me about Majellan. Why does he hate my family?"

"I lost the Adularia stone. Do you have it?" he asked. I flashed back to our meeting and the stone rolling under the dryer in the laundry room. I'd completely forgotten about it.

"No."

"Good. That's good. It will never be found by Majellan." He sighed heavily, shut his weary eyes. "The Raturro have long awaited your return. The prophecy is true."

"What prophecy?"

"My people have passed a prophecy down for generations." He coughed and sputtered. "It was told you would free all Raturro. We have looked forward to your return. '*The Last Murch will save us all.*'"

"I don't think your prophecy was talking about me. I've been on Earth for a long time. You're the only Raturro I've ever met."

"For now, you are the last in the Murch line. Only you can save us."

"No, you're wrong about me. I have no idea how to help," I said.

"I only wanted to warn you, bring you to safety," he said.

"Um, I'm sorry about the electricity thing." I raised my arm and did a pretend zap. "I didn't mean to—"

"I know, child," he whispered, his breathing shallow.

"Where's Majellan?" I asked again. "I need to talk to him. He has my mom. A hostage."

"Impossible," he whimpered.

"I saw it. He took her."

"The Queen?" Shale seemed puzzled. "He has the Queen?"

"No, my mom. Oh, yeah, I guess she is a queen. I don't know why she didn't tell me." This place was so weird. "Do you know where she is, Shale? I have to find her."

He moaned as a wave of pain shuddered through him then he coughed uncontrollably. "Oh, Ko-ru-ku, my children... you must help them," he sobbed. Large tears soaked his furry face. Then he rolled himself into a little ball and his thick rat-tail wrapped around him. "I beg you, save my children, Ko-ru-ku," he whispered.

"Ko-ru-ku? What does that mean? Shale? I don't understand. Who did this to you?"

He went quiet. His pink tail softened and uncoiled.

"Mr. Raturro?" I craned my neck to see if he was breathing, but he was still. Scared, I jumped back from the cell. There was a burning in my chest and the tears welled up in my eyes. No, this couldn't be happening. "Shale? Wake up!"

Shale didn't move. He was dead and there was nothing I could do. I ran back up the sloping tunnel and stopped. I'd never seen anyone die before. Why did I feel so sad for the rat-man? Dad was at war with him and the Raturro. Majellan took my mom. But Shale cried for his children.

I ran up to the next level, unsure where I was. I turned a corner and ran right into Sergeant Talia. "Your father's been looking for you," she said.

"Uh, I'm tired. I want to go to my room," I said, afraid I couldn't look my father in the eye. Grudgingly, she escorted me back and I threw myself on the bed.

"Ko-ru-ku," I whispered. I couldn't get that word out of my head. Why would Shale have said all those things to me? I didn't believe in his prophecy. That sounded impossible. I didn't know how to save the Raturro. The poor man…er… rat. He was tortured and punished for trying to find me. It was my fault he was captured. I should have asked to see him sooner. I could have gotten the doctor to help him.

Then an awful thought came into my head: Did Dad give the order to torture Shale? Did Dad kill Shale?

I hated this place and didn't want to be here anymore. I thought it would be so great to see Dad again, but it was becoming so complicated. And horrible. I thought back, long and hard, to when I was a little girl. I didn't remember it very well, but I knew there was a happy time that I shared with my parents. I pulled the photo from my pocket and examined it closely—the monkey-puzzle tree, that was a real place. I was sure of it. We were happy. But not so much anymore.

Murch. I was starting to hate my name.

The next morning, I awoke early and got dressed. I was tying my laces when Dad came to the door.

"I'm sorry about last night," I said to my shoes, not sure if I really meant it. "I just can't believe this place. It's so different. I miss Mom. I miss home." I couldn't meet his eye. "I want to go back."

"Kyra, there's no going back. This is your home now."

He didn't really mean it. He couldn't.

"But I can't stay here," I said trying to keep my voice steady.

He didn't ask why.

The Mess Hall was packed and everyone stood up and saluted. "At ease," Dad said and everyone sat down. I shifted uncomfortably; all eyes were upon me. I couldn't stop thinking about Shale. He was dead, and I couldn't help him. I watched Dad as he spoke, looking for a hint of the cruelty that was needed to kill another living thing.

"I know some of you have already heard that my daughter Kyra has joined us. I wanted to officially introduce her to you. She is heir to the throne of Antiica and is to be protected at any cost." His eyes were serious and made contact with many of the soldiers who nodded solemnly. "She is the future of our world. The future for all humans." A cheer went up in the hall, and I jumped in surprise. Dad put his hand on my shoulder. It was all I could do not to pull away. Dad turned to give me a chance to speak but tears stung my eyes instead.

"We have some grave days ahead," he continued. "The Queen has been captured."

The soldiers gasped in shock.

Dad took a moment before continuing. "But we will get her back. The Raturro have driven all humans out of Murch City. But we will win it back. Your homes will be returned to you. Your families will be reunited. You have my solemn word." Another cheer erupted and Dad allowed a half-smile. They all loved and respected him. He was their leader, and I knew right then I could never be like him.

As we ate, soldiers passed by our table and saluted me. I forced a smile back and Dad nodded his appreciation to me. "You will be a good queen one day," he said.

"Me?" I blurted, nearly choking on my meat. I gulped down a glass of pink juice, trying to clear my throat. "I don't ever want to do that."

"There are some things in life that we can't choose. Our birthright. Our responsibilities. It's an honour to serve." He looked proud, commanding, but he felt less like my father every moment.

"Why is Sergeant Talia still guarding me?" I asked.

"I just want you to feel safe. You've been through a lot and she can help you get to know the Armory," he said. "But if you think you'd be better on your own…."

I gave what I hoped was a convincing smile to conceal the sinking feeling in my heart. I couldn't stop thinking about Shale and the possibility that Dad had killed him. No, it was no longer a possibility. Shale was a prisoner. Dad either killed him or had him killed.

After breakfast I was restless, so I wandered around the Armory watching soldiers work. I came across a gymnasium where young soldiers were learning combat skills. Basic training. There were some boys and girls in there that were so young and small I couldn't imagine them fighting giant rats and living to tell about it. I shuddered and backed away.

Dad was still working so I took lunch in my room, and I was afraid I'd blurt out something about Shale. Dad was obsessed with his war, and I didn't want to be a part of it.

"*Kyraaa,*" her soft voice called to me.

"Huh?" I jumped up from my bed. I didn't know what to do. Was I supposed to go when the chimera called?

As I made my way towards the cavern where I last saw her, I passed a series of windows that looked down on the Concourse and saw Dad standing atop a tank, barking orders at soldiers. Right at that moment, as if he sensed me there, he turned and looked straight at me. I quickly turned away, pretending I didn't see him. A feeling of panic washed through me and I realized how badly I wanted to go home. I knew it was impossible, but maybe Mom was back now. Maybe she had escaped and was at home waiting for me. I held onto that belief as I picked up the pace and ran to the cavern.

The chimera was still sleeping when I burst into the room. "Chimera?" No response. I timidly approached her, concentrated again, said the word in my head: *Chimera!* But she didn't light up. All I could hear were my own worried thoughts—what about Mom?

I slapped the wall hard with my hand. Nothing.

"Chimera, take me home," I said aloud.

Home? She purred inside my head.

Even though I had a sudden blast of pain from the chimera's intrusion, I was excited. She had listened to me. I did it. I breathed deeply, trying to make the pain subside.

Kyraaa, she whispered again and the cavern was flooded with light.

"Take me home," I said, louder this time. I didn't want to be at the Armory. I couldn't get the thought of Shale dying in front of me out of my head.

"Kyra! Wait! What're you doing?" said Dad, who had suddenly entered the cavern.

"I don't belong here. I'm going home," I said.

"You can't leave. It's too dangerous and you're not properly trained to interact with the chimera."

"I don't care!"

"This base is the safest place on Antiica right now. There's a war going on out there. It's not just on Antiica, it's carried over onto Earth now. The enemy will never rest until they find you, Kyra. You're in grave danger," he echoed Shale's warning.

I hesitated. Would the Raturro really be waiting for me if I returned to Earth?

"You have a duty to your people," he continued.

"They're not my people. I don't want to be heir to anything. I saw Shale. He's dead. Did you kill him?"

Dad hesitated just enough to let me know he was responsible. "You don't understand. You don't know what the Raturro have done to our people. Majellan is a murderer and he must be stopped." His voice took on a dull echoey quality. It was softer, quieter, filtered out by something in my head. Then there was a buzzing, a vibration, a rising ache.

Without realizing it, I had inched closer to the chimera. Like a siren, she was calling to me and somehow I had to answer. I could go away for a little while and then come back. I wasn't sure where the chimera could take me, but I had no choice. I knew she needed me. I knew I needed her just as much. Time slowed down again. I was melting backwards, shocked that I was leaving, but also feeling like I could burst out laughing. The last thing I heard was Dad's voice.

"Kyra, no!"

Then I fell backwards into the void.

Chapter Six

I thought I had held my breath, but I woke up on my back on a rough, hard-packed mud floor. It wasn't the laundry room. I was still in the Armory. I had failed.

As I tried to move, waves of pain sailed through my head. I moaned and shut my eyes again. I had come through the chimera, but instead of feeling warmth and safety, it seemed like I'd jumped through a ring of fire. I could even smell smoke. I opened my eyes again. "I'm okay," I said aloud, expecting Dad to run over, but I was alone.

"Hello? Chimera?" I whispered, still unsure of my surroundings. The chimera was a dark line engraved on a stone wall in front of me. I listened for her voice. Nothing. She had left my head. Where was I?

Embers glowed in a small fireplace. I was in a tiny cottage built from large, white round stones, with a ceiling of crisscrossed wooden beams and a roof made out of blackened straw. Dust and cobwebs covered the walls. There was no furniture, just a tiny three-legged stool which lay broken in the corner. This definitely wasn't the Armory. Where was I?

I was woozy, and as I stood unsteadily I bashed my head on the low ceiling. The cottage was too small for me. It was like I was inside some sort of doll's house.

"What are we doing here?" I said.

The chimera lit up on the wall behind me. Her six eyes beamed fiery red. *This is as close to home as we could take you,* she purred.

"Huh?" I jumped, not expecting her to answer and bumped my head again.

You told us to come here. Home.

"Ow! You're shouting!" I grabbed my head, melting back down to the floor.

The dragon head lit up the room as it snaked out of the wall and hovered above me. I shrank down, wary, as the dragon watched me with bright red eyes, unsure if she would strike.

"Where are we?" I finally managed in a shaky whisper.

"*This is as close to Murch City as we can go. We cannot take you directly into the city,*" she murmured to me.

"We're near Murch City?" I asked. "Why?"

"*You asked us to take you to your mother. You asked for home.*"

"I did?" The dragon shrunk back into the wall and started to dim. "No, wait," I cried frantically. "Let's go back to the Armory. I've made a big mistake." I ran for the chimera's fading light but hit the stone wall instead, landing on the floor.

"Ow, what did you do that for, you dumb monster?!" I rubbed my aching knee.

"*We followed your heart's desire. You asked us to find your mother and that is what you want the most. Your mother's in Thane's Reach,*" she said.

"She is? What's Thane's Reach? Is it near here?" I asked.

"Thane's Reach is your ancestral home in the heart of Murch City."

So I was close enough to help Mom. I really wanted to see her, and I knew she'd take me back home to Earth. I wobbled to my feet, dusted myself off.

"So what're we waiting for? Let's go and get her."

"We can't enter Thane's Reach."

"Why not?" I raised my voice. This was so frustrating. I couldn't understand this thing at all.

"We have a security protocol. We are locked out of Thane's Reach."

"I don't understand."

"Our bond keeps us alive. Without you, Kyraaa, we will cease to be."

"You need me?" I asked, surprised. "You've got all these crazy powers. I can't do anything."

"We are one," she replied. The chimera slowly dimmed to a dark outline on the wall.

"Come back, you stupid beast," I yelled, but she didn't listen. I went to the wall and slapped it, but she never lit up. "Are you listening to me? Come back. Now!"

Nothing.

"That's an order," I said weakly. I was either being ignored or speaking the wrong language. There was a growing emptiness inside of me. I'd never missed Mom so much in my whole life.

"Chimera?" I leaned my head against her outline on the wall. "Please." But she didn't answer. What had I done?

Suddenly the door flew open and a bitter-cold wind blew in. A tall boy was in the doorway, a bucket of sand in his hand, looking every bit as surprised as I was. He wasn't much older than me. He had bright, hazel eyes, warm honey skin. His curly dark hair was pitted with bits of leaves and grass.

"What're you doing here?" he asked suspiciously, looking me over.

I was so startled I couldn't even blurt out a lie. I just stood there and shivered like a dork. He kicked the door shut.

"You can't stay here." He threw the sand over the fire, smothering it. Beneath his long, shabby brown coat, I glimpsed army fatigues, ripped and caked with old mud. Was he a soldier in my father's army?

Chimera, where are you? No answer.

"Are you a soldier?" I asked boldly.

"Who's asking?" He poked at the fire, made sure it was out. "War is dumb." He turned to face me, pulled his coat tighter around him. He searched my face, then warned, "But if you need a soldier, there's plenty around here."

Could my father be far behind?

"I need to get to Murch City. Can you show me the way?"

He laughed out loud and my heart sunk a little. "That's impossible. You can't go near the city. It's fallen to the Raturro."

"I'm not afraid of the Raturro."

He shook his head. "You should be."

It was at that moment the chimera lit up the room. I felt a lightning bolt of pain between my eyes, and my mind was invaded with a sudden uncontrollable rage. Before I knew what had happened, I dove at the boy. I grabbed his arm and flipped him down onto the hard floor. It was a quick, fluid motion that happened without any effort. In just a few seconds, I was standing over him, my tight fist pointed like a weapon at his face. The chimera had taken over my body.

Again. This thing had a power over me and I really didn't know how to control it. It didn't make any sense, and I was beginning to hate it.

But the look of surprise on his face almost made me laugh. He really wasn't expecting me to take him down. Neither was I. My heart was racing. I was out of control. Then the chimera dimmed; my strength ebbed away. I was the same as I'd always been.

Awkward.

What was I doing?

"Uh, I'm so sorry. Are you okay?" I said.

He looked at me like I was a monster, and then he glanced over at the chimera with real fear in his eyes.

"I need you to take me into the city. Thane's Reach—that's where my mom is. It's really important that I find her." We locked eyes and I recognized a look of determination in him.

"Or what? You'll get your monster to fry me?" he asked.

We stared at each other for a moment longer and then I finally stood back.

He sat up and the sudden movement caused me to jump. "Uh, I'm not going to hurt you."

"Obviously," I said.

He glanced at the chimera. "Why can't that thing take you to Thane's Reach? That's what it's for, isn't it?"

"How do you know?"

He laughed again, but I could tell he knew more than he was saying. "Thane's Reach. That's where the rebels have set up camp. It's impenetrable."

"The rebels?" I asked.

"Big rats? Huge claws? Mortal enemies of the Kingdom of Antiica?" he said, incredulous.

"Oh. There must be a way in," I said. I envisioned the chimera in my mind and asked her the same question. *Chimera?* No response.

"Look, no human can get inside the perimeter because it's so heavily guarded. They have weapons. Lots of weapons. If your mom is there, well, I don't think anyone can help her." He pointed at the chimera. "Not even that thing."

"I don't care. I'm going anyway," I insisted.

He stared at me a moment, grit his teeth, then sighed heavily. "I'm heading close to Fuuto Point. You can tag along if you want, but that's as far as I go. I don't know any other way inside the Reach, and I sure don't want to get caught trying," the boy said, a gleam in his eye. It was almost a challenge, and I could swear he suddenly looked taller.

"Fuuto Point." I nodded. I had no idea where it was. "Yeah, that'll do."

"So, what kind of soldier are you?" he asked.

"Me? As if!" I laughed, feeling suddenly awkward in the cramped house.

"I'm Coyne," he said, breaking our stalemate.

"Uh, I'm Kyra," I stammered.

"Of course you are," he chuckled, now confident. He turned to the door, stooped down and went out into the day. The light momentarily blinded me, and I fumbled over to put my hands on the cold, stone wall.

"Chimera? Are you in there? What should I do? Chimera?" I whispered.

No response.

"Are you coming, or are you going to talk to the wall all day?" Coyne called from outside. He had seen me. Now I felt like a complete dork.

My hands fell from the wall. I needed to figure out this chimera thing—why was it so hard? But if she wasn't listening to me, I didn't know what else to do. She wouldn't take me home. She wouldn't take me into Murch City. I felt the push-pull of her inside my head. I wanted her with me but at the same time I didn't. I shuddered. She was a monster, after all.

Thane's Reach. I could get there on my own. Could I trust Coyne to help me? I realized I had no choice. So I stooped down and made my way through the small wooden door, hoping I was doing the right thing.

The brightness of the day surprised me, but there was still a cool wind. We were on a farm in the middle of the countryside. It was green and sunny surrounded by overgrown fields of grass and shrubbery, and after years of living in a big city it seemed like an alien landscape to me. This was Antiica. Even though the farm had been abandoned, there were still a few remnants of farm life. There was a very small, dilapidated wagon that must have had a very small horse pulling it sometime in the past, and a tiny rope swing hung from the hugest tree I'd ever seen, over near the barn. It was quaint, but there was also something so sad about it. I suddenly thought about Shale and how he cried for his children.

"Let's go." Coyne was restless, and despite what he said, I recognized the soldier in him. He paced, watched for movement, fingers clenched. He led me away from the farm, down a winding road. Then we veered off into a forest of thin, white trees with long weepy tendrils of moss for leaves. I ran my hands over the soft moss and wanted to bury my face in it.

As the sun rose higher in the sky, it got hotter and hotter. I took off my jacket and tied it around my waist. Soon, we stopped by a stream and drank heavily. I wondered if this was the same sun that shone down on Earth.

"You'll need some food for the journey. You can get supplies at Fuuto Point," Coyne said as he refilled his flask.

"That farm we were on, why was everything so small? The cottage, the wagon, it all looked like it was made for children," I asked.

Coyne looked at me a moment, thinking. "You don't know?"

"I really don't know anything about Antiica."

"Where've you been?" He grinned. "The Moons of Juris?"

"Pretty close," I said, even though I had no idea what he was talking about.

"All this land belonged to the Raturro. You know what *they* are?" he asked sarcastically.

"The rat-men."

"More rat than man. That's why everything's so small. The Raturro from this area are the smallest of all. Not like the city Raturro, or even the ones down south. I've never seen them, but they're supposed to be eight feet tall and can bite the head off a serpent."

"Serpent?"

"We'd better get moving. You never know when the Raturro will show up. They've got a keen sense of smell and claws that can tear the flesh right off you. We're on the human side of the front. The Raturro have the city and we're all forced into the country. That's not the way it used to be, but since the rebellion...."

I shuddered. I didn't want to run into the Raturro, but I couldn't stop thinking about Shale and the prophecy. Why would he even think I could save them? Save them from what?

"Ko-ru-ku," I said out loud. Coyne looked at me warily. "Have you heard this word, Ko-ru-ku?"

Coyne screwed the lid on his flask and slipped it into a fold in his coat. He shook his head no. Then he just walked off, an aura of confidence about him. I began to doubt Coyne's motives and my own. I'd hastily decided to follow this stranger out into a land full of rats with sharp claws waiting to rip us to shreds. And why was he so eager to help me?

"Uh, wait. What did you say about serpents? Wait up."

He grinned slyly back at me, and I wasn't sure if anything he said was the truth.

As we walked through grass taller than the both of us, I thought about the chimera. She was made of light but only traveled through stone, so if I wanted her help I was going to need to find another stone wall. Maybe just a rock face or a large boulder? I wondered if the chimera could fly through the air; it had wings. Maybe we could zoom over Murch City and rescue Mom that way. It sounded ridiculous, but strange things were no longer out of the ordinary. I was on another planet, wandering the alien landscape with a stranger.

Coyne came running back towards me. "Quick, this way," he whispered. "Patrol." He pointed back the way he'd come. I hesitated, but he grabbed my arm and dragged me to a copse of trees we had just passed. We dove behind some fallen trees. Could rats hear you breathe?

After a few moments, I pulled my hands off my face. I didn't want to look, didn't want to see the Raturro, and couldn't get the idea of their sharp claws digging into my flesh out of my mind. Coyne gave me a look of understanding. He then pointed to a little gap between the fallen tree trunks we were lodged behind. But instead of Raturro, it was a patrol of human soldiers.

Was Dad searching for me? I couldn't go back to the Armory. Then I realized it was far too soon and he couldn't possibly know where I'd gone. I didn't even know where I was. But, if the soldiers weren't searching for me, then who were they looking for?

When they were out of sight, Coyne breathed a big sigh of relief.

"Who are they looking for? You? Are you an army deserter?" I wondered out loud, but he shrugged it off.

"If we get caught," he whispered, "remember, you kidnapped me."

"Kidnapped?"

"Isn't someone missing a princess?" he joked.

"Don't know what you're talking about."

He smirked at me. "You're the daughter of the Thane, aren't you? I'm sure he wouldn't like it if you were wandering a few leagues from Raturro territory. He must have sent his goons out for you. I should've handed you over. There might be a reward."

"Reward?" I raised my voice.

"Shhhhh!" he whispered and ducked back down. "The Thane is the ruler, you know, the supreme being."

"You have the wrong person." I had heard Dad referred to as Thane back at the Armory but wasn't sure if I could trust Coyne with the knowledge.

"There's only one Kyra Murch," he said, reaching deep into his coat pocket. I winced. Was it a weapon? But he pulled out a battered brown leather wallet. Inside was a worn photo of my parents in royal regalia and me, about four years old, at their side. Behind them on the wall was the outline of the chimera, a huge dark coat-of-arms.

It was strange looking at the photo, at this whole other life I couldn't remember. I'd never even seen that photo before but there was something familiar about it. I vaguely remembered tugging on the shiny silk of Mom's dress, the rustle as she leaned down and promised me something if I'd stand still and let the camera take our photo. I felt her soft hand on my cheek, the warmth of her breath by my ear, her floral perfume.

"Everyone has this photo. It was a tradition of your parents to bestow them on the peasants once a year. My mom has a larger version over the fireplace," he teased.

I flushed, embarrassed. My parents had kept me in the dark all my life. Then I giggled at the ridiculousness of it all. There was a sudden movement in the trees behind us. Leaves rustled and the hair on the back of my neck stood up. Coyne and I had been laughing about the stupid picture; we'd let our guard down. As we both turned to the sound, expecting soldiers to burst out of the forest, I had no idea what we'd drawn to us. The realization that we were in the middle of a war zone hit me. There was danger all around us and we were going to have to deal with it or face the consequences.

CHAPTER SEVEN

Coyne and I both held our breath, expecting the worst, and then a large furry creature emerged from the trees. It was as big as a sheep, with long black shaggy fur, but had a face like a wise old pig. It snorted in our direction and then trotted past us and disappeared between thorny shrubs.

"Harmless," whispered Coyne, but I was still worried. Giant rats and huge hairy pigs. What else would we find? Oh, and serpents. He mentioned serpents.

"Now what do we do?" I whispered back, still frightened by the prospect of meeting the Raturro out in the middle of nowhere. There was no place to hide.

"Well, princess," he said with a mischievous grin, "the longer we sit here the longer it will take to get to Fuuto Point."

"They're looking for you too, aren't they?"

"No, they're searching for Raturro. They don't care about me. I guarantee it." He stood up, tall, as if daring those soldiers to take him in.

I decided to drop it. He might run off and then I'd be lost for sure. I needed him to get me to Murch City. It was so weird. I *was* some sort of princess. Ugh! Princesses were for fairy tales and little kids who believed in fantasy.

We walked in silence for a few hours through fields and along paths, avoiding bombed out farms and villages. The closer we got to Fuuto, the worse the damage was. I was glad that Coyne avoided the villages where there had been some serious fighting. We kept to the back roads and tried not to call attention to ourselves. One time we found some fresh tracks, but they were from army boots not giant rat claws. Human, but still it worried me. If we encountered a patrol, they would stop us from going anywhere near Murch. But a little part of me was glad there was protection out there somewhere. After we'd trudged dusty paths and dry gullies and climbed over rocky walls and down steep embankments for most of the day, I was tired and my stomach growled.

"What do you know about Majellan, the rebel leader?"

"I know that I never want to meet him. Majellan was the one who started the rebellion. It was slow at first, just a few Raturro refusing to work. Then Majellan and his buddies started sabotaging food sources and killing humans. I never trusted those rats. Not like some people did. Had them living in their houses, working for them, watching their children. Disgusting," he continued. "I don't see what's so great about having servants anyway. Back on the Plains where I'm from, most people don't want them around. We do our own work." He stopped a moment, looked off into the horizon. "It's pretty there. Yellow samarlia fields as far as the eye can see. The summers are hot, much hotter than this. You work hard at harvest time, but it feels good to know you're feeding people."

The sunlight flecked in his eyes and I couldn't help but stare at him. He really wasn't meant to be a soldier. He was a farm boy through and through.

"What?" he asked.

"Huh? Oh, nothing," I stammered. "Uh, what about Thane's Reach? How long will it take me to get there?"

"It's hard to say. Depends on where the Raturro pick you up and how long it takes to drag you behind them in chains," he chuckled.

"How long?"

He gave me a goofy shrug. My idea to save Mom now sounded impossible. I was tired of hearing about all the bad things the Raturro did. I still couldn't believe I was on this weird planet with talking rats. And following a farm boy into the wilderness.

"I have to find my mom," I said loudly.

"Shhhh!" he said, his eyes darting about. He signaled me to get down and we squatted in the long grass. I strained my ears but didn't hear anything out of the ordinary. But then I realized it was dead quiet. No birdsong or buzz of insects. That usually meant trouble, right?

Coyne peeked up over the long grass and signaled me to get up. We crept to a line of trees and sat in the shade, waiting. A trickle of sweat ran down my back. My feet were raw with blisters, my leg muscles aching. I'd never walked so much in my entire life and I was dying to pull off my runners.

I was relieved to hear the birdsong start up again. "What was it?"

Coyne whispered, "Something looking for its dinner."

"Oh," I said. At least it wasn't hunting us. Maybe we could learn from the birds and be a bit quieter.

Coyne continued, "It's not far to Fuuto, but we should look for a place to spend the night. We don't want to go into a village in the darkness. They'll have guards." We got up on our feet, followed the tree line and then slipped down a gully to a small creek where we found a hidden spot to camp. I splashed cool water on my dusty face and guzzled down the sweet water. Coyne pulled off his heavy coat and boots and stuck his feet in the creek. I threw off my runners and did the same. We sat there staring at our tired red feet. My stomach gurgled loudly and even Coyne noticed.

He crawled over to a patch of long, leafy plants and dug out purple, red, and orange tubers that looked like stubby fat carrots. While I washed them in the creek, I was startled to see him starting a fire.

"What are you doing? Someone will see the smoke!" I said.

"Nah, sun's going down. It's hazy. There's a bit of wind from that ridge over there carrying the smoke away."

I gazed around us. I hadn't noticed any of that, but he knew the area. I felt suddenly confident that he could get me into Murch City, if only I could persuade him.

We put the tubers in the fire, and, when they were done, extinguished the flames with sand from the creek. The tubers tasted like dirt and grass, but I gobbled them down anyway. The skies grew dark and there was no telling who was lurking in the nearby hills. We sat in the darkness and Coyne spoke of his family again.

"Calley's the youngest. She's just eight years old. Hm. Maybe nine now. Full of fun and always plays jokes on everyone. She's a hard worker though, loves to help with the chores around the farm. Then there's Asha. She's eleven. Very quiet, thoughtful, likes to write everything down in a book. She'd go to school forever if she could. And then there's Spite."

"Spite? Who names their kid Spite?"

"Spite's real name is Kornelia, but she didn't like it at all. She was always kind of mean to Asha, and Mom said she was spiteful. So she changed it to Spite. She was probably tired of my calling her Kornie."

"And your mom just calls her that?"

"No, not so much, but we all do. It's funny. You kind of remind me of Spite," he said, and I knew he was teasing me.

His life on the Plains sounded so quaint, so happy. I knew now why he was risking his life to get home. "It sounds like you really miss them, Coyne."

He nodded.

"I miss my mom so much. And she's in danger. I don't know how I'm going to rescue her when I get to Murch, but I know I can't do it alone."

"Kyra, I told you, I can only go to Fuuto Point. Even that isn't safe. If I don't get home, the farm will lose its crop. They need me."

"But what if you could save the Queen of Antiica?" I asked. If he carried that photo of my family he must feel some loyalty to them.

"Let's get some rest." Coyne rolled over and was soon snoring, but I couldn't get to sleep. Every sound, every movement had me on edge. There were Raturro out there somewhere and we were easy prey.

I was soon mesmerized by not one but three moons rising like emerald beacons above me. Were these the Moons of Juris? They did kind of look like Earth's moon. One was big, closer to Antiica, and the other two were about half the size, like little sisters tagging along behind. I jumped when

Coyne grumbled in his sleep. I had no idea how he could sleep when danger lurked nearby. I thought of the way he spoke about his family and I wished I had a brother or sister. I could've used their help.

Coyne was already up when I awoke at dawn. He shared his water flask with me and even though the leftover roots were cold they tasted much better than the night before. "So, how far to Fuuto?" I asked him.

He pointed to the biggest hill in front of us, on the other side of the creek. "See that hill? We'll climb up there and hopefully, it's still on the other side."

"Why wouldn't it be?"

"The rebels have been burning down all the towns between here and the city. We'll go down into the town and I can ask around for you. See if the road to Murch is clear. Get a sense of things."

"Okay." I nodded.

"So what's your plan?" he asked.

"I'll see if someone in Fuuto can lead me to Murch."

"You got any money to pay somebody?" I shook my head, no. He clucked. "So what's your plan, princess?"

I stood up, shook the sand off my jeans and set off toward the hill that stood between me and Fuuto Point. Behind me, Coyne sighed but followed anyway.

Coyne and I climbed the hill covered in a dry brittle grass that poked my bare ankles. He signaled me to get down. We crawled forward on our elbows and gazed down on a small village nestled in a greenbelt, a patchwork of farmland and forests beyond. Fuuto seemed untouched by the war. A haven.

"That's Fuuto Point," Coyne said. We sat and watched the village for a while, making sure there were no Raturro or soldiers milling about. Then Coyne said, "So, you're sure the queen is in Thane's Reach?"

"Yes." My stomach fluttered with excitement. Was he going to come with me?

He pointed past the valley to a small mountain. "The city of Murch is on the other side of that mountain."

I was close. The chimera had brought me much closer than I realized. "Let's go," I said and jumped to my feet. He flashed one of his mischievous grins and we started walking down the other side of the hill towards the village.

"I don't get it. How can you tell which Raturro are the rebels?" I asked as we lumbered down the steep hill.

"There's Majellan's army—the original rebels. They're huge, dark grey city Raturro. You can spot them from a league away. At least two heads taller than me. They're big and they're fast. They can rip your throat out before you even realize they've touched you. The other races of Raturro are smaller, lighter coloured. Some are multi-coloured. But any Raturro could be a rebel spy just dying to turn you in for a reward. So you can't trust any of them."

"Are there any nice Raturro on Antiica?" I asked, thinking of Shale.

"They're all the enemy. Never forget that." He grimly pointed to the village ahead. "Just because we can't see the enemy doesn't mean they aren't there."

The quaint village had houses with thatched wooden roofs. It was like a postcard photo of an English countryside village I'd once seen in a textbook. Surely something so pretty couldn't be anything bad.

CHAPTER EIGHT

By the time we reached the village I was starving and hoped that we could eat soon. Maybe we could find a restaurant and order something deep-fried, like chicken or fries or anything with some grease on it. And ketchup. I had a sudden craving for ketchup.

The village was truly an odd place. It appeared quaint from afar but up close I saw rough stone houses with roofs made of sticks and mud and people dressed in rags.

"Let's keep our heads down," said Coyne.

I nodded but couldn't help all the questions I had. "How come it's so old-fashioned here?" I murmured.

"Old-fashioned? What do you mean?"

"Well, there aren't any cars or even lights in the streets," I said, glancing around.

Coyne looked at me strangely. "I don't know what you mean."

"Uh, technology? You know, computers and TVs and stuff? My father has—" I stopped. Maybe I shouldn't tell him what I'd seen in the Armory. Maybe he had never been there before. Then I had a terrible thought. If there were Raturro spies, couldn't there be human spies too?

"Your father has what?"

"Uh, nothing. Forget it," I said.

We slipped down a narrow street and came out in the middle of a town square where a few tables were set up to sell food. We kept to the fringes, and I let Coyne lead me through the throng of people. They were wary of us. Strangers. They stared, but I avoided their eyes.

The square was filled with old men and women with small children. They wandered around buying what little food was available at the stalls. Some of the men were typical farmers with old coveralls and ripped shirts, the odd worn hat, but there were also men who looked like they didn't belong. They wore army fatigues and had missing limbs and crutches. Some of them just sat and stared into space. I wondered if any of them could be spies.

The women were all old and tired with grey hair and saggy dresses. They were nothing like Mom, and I wondered who the small children belonged to. The children were without shoes, dirty with runny noses and tear-streaked faces. They reminded me of characters in a book I'd once loved, *Oliver Twist*. It was the story of an orphan who gets in with a bad crowd of thieving children. I was beginning to think that, like Oliver, I'd trusted Coyne a little too much and was in over my head.

"Why are all these people so poor, so hungry?"

Coyne stopped at a stall heaped high with gnarled brown fuzzy fruit. He glared at me. "Sorry if it doesn't live up to your expectations, *princess*. Like I've been saying—there's a war on." He glanced around at the old women chatting nearby and then Coyne expertly slipped a few of the fruits into his pocket.

What was he doing? All these people were poor, struggling through a war, and now he was stealing from them? Before I could utter a word he grabbed my arm and led me over to a public well, which was just a small pipe supported by a limestone wall. He filled his flask and pointed to a bashed tin cup that sat on a high ledge.

"You're kidding, right?" With a grimace, I reached for the grubby cup.

"Hide that!" He yanked my jacket sleeve down over my bracelet, which popped out when I reached for the cup. "People are starting to notice us. We can't have them asking us any questions."

"About my bracelet?" He didn't answer.

A trickle of brown water came out of the spout and I half-filled the cup and choked down the rusty tasting liquid. I guessed there weren't going to be any fast food restaurants in my immediate future. "Are all the kids our age fighting the Raturro?"

He nodded and his face clouded over. "That old man over there, he's staring at us," whispered Coyne. "You don't want to tell people around here who you are, understand? When you're hungry enough, you're easily bought."

I wondered how hungry Coyne was. Was he leading me into a trap? No, I had to trust him. He could've turned me over to the soldiers we passed the day before. Coyne was my only hope to get into Murch.

There was a sudden buzzing in my brain and then Majellan's ugly visage flashed in front of me. It wasn't the recurring vision. This was new. He was standing up in a moving wood wagon, surrounded by Raturro soldiers.

Coyne stared at me, "Are you all right?"

I nodded but was worried about the vision. What did it mean? I placed my hand on the limestone wall but felt nothing. What if I couldn't find the chimera again?

I was about to mention my vision when Coyne ushered me away from the well. As we walked we scanned the crowd and spotted the old man just as he turned to speak to a tall, menacing guy with a huge scar down his cheek and missing part of his jaw. He nudged a stooped man who leant on a crutch next to him. All three stared back at us.

"You there," the tall one called as he approached.

Coyne and I veered into the throng of people, but the man shouted. "Have you news of the war?" The crowd of people ahead turned to see what was happening. We were trapped. The tall man grabbed Coyne by the shoulder and spun him around.

"I was talking to you, boy. What news do you have?"

"None, sir," replied Coyne, his usual joking manner serious now. "I'm on my way back to the Plains. My family needs me for the harvest."

The three men were right beside us, and Coyne waved me behind him. "So you've been relieved of duty, have you?" said the old man, who watched me closely.

Coyne nodded brusquely. "The Thane needs us to keep food production up, so my friend and I are going home to the Plains."

"A bit far from home, aren't you?" The old man wouldn't let up.

"We had to avoid Raturro patrols. They're everywhere."

The old man thought about it for a moment and then advanced a few steps trying to get a better look at me. "You know what we do with deserters around here?" the old man continued.

"Yes, sir," said Coyne standing erect like a soldier. I cowered behind him but couldn't escape the prying looks of the townspeople. Should have covered up my pink hair.

The old man wouldn't stop. "What news do you have from the front?"

"The rebels have gained more ground and all of Murch City has fallen. There's a battle in the east. You'd best move up to the mountains while you still can," said Coyne.

"Like cowards?" The men around him grumbled.

Just then a group of old women passed behind us and I pulled Coyne towards them. We managed to meld into their group until a sturdy wooden wagon drove in front of us forcing everyone to stop. A terrible cracking sound made me jump. Painful whimpers erupted ahead, and I could see the human driver viciously whipping two emaciated, dark grey Raturro who were pulling the wagon.

There was much jostling and chatting around me, but I pushed forward to get a better look. The Raturro's panting and whimpers grew louder as they trotted past within inches of me. As the stench of sweat and oil wafted around me, I held my breath. I winced remembering Shale and his suffering in the dungeon of the Armory. It wasn't right.

Hunched in the back of the wooden wagon were two light grey Raturro. One was a muscular male, the other a sad girl in a dirty dress. The hair on the back of my neck pricked up. I was sure I had seen her someplace before, but that would be impossible.

The wagon veered through the crowd and pulled up beside a platform that was set up in the middle of the square. The Raturro girl was roughly pulled out of the back of the wagon, her paws shackled with heavy chains, but she held her head high in defiance as she was pushed up onto the rickety platform.

Coyne was lost in the throng of people. I panicked, trying to catch a glimpse of him, but the crowd pushed me towards the platform.

Ahead of me, the wagon driver roughly pushed the male Raturro towards the female Raturro. The crowd broke out in loud chanting and jeering. But as a weather-beaten old woman clambered up to join them on the platform, the crowd hushed. She made her way to the centre of the stage, gazed out over the crowd. I continued scanning the crowd for Coyne. Where was he?

"We have four Raturro for sale here today. Does anyone else want to sell a slave?" she stated matter-of-factly. I recoiled. The Raturro were slaves? She glanced over the crowd waiting for a response, and a voice soon cried out, "Two here." The two scrawnier underfed Raturro were pushed up onto the platform.

The crowd pushed me forward again.

"All right," the old woman continued. "These two first. A hundred a head. They go as a pair. De-clawed."

The owner of the two Raturro signaled them to hold up their paws, and I grimaced at the grisly sight. Their claws had been removed leaving only stumps, just like Shale's. I scanned the arms and legs of the Raturro and saw scars where they'd been whipped. A lump rose in my throat and I tried to retreat, but the crowd of villagers jostled me forward.

"Forty," a shout rang out from the crowd.

"Forty-five." Another shout.

"Oh, come on, lads. These are two strong rats. They're only sixteen years old. Young-uns."

"Sixty."

"Seventy-five."

The crowd grumbled.

"Any other bids? Last chance." No one added to the bids. "Sold," she shouted. The man led the Raturro off towards the side of the platform, and the buyer placed heavy leashes around their necks and yanked them tight.

The Raturro girl was brought forward to the front of the platform. She hung her head, defeated. The old woman called out to the crowd, "Female, farm worker, about thirteen." She grabbed the girl's shackled paws and held them up. They still had their claws attached. "Obedient, still has her claws, good worker. Two hundred."

The crowd murmured in surprise.

"No slave's worth that," someone called.

The old woman shrugged.

"Fifty," started the bids.

I eyed the crowd again for Coyne. Where was he? A surge from the crowd pushed me right up against the wooden platform. I pushed back against a woman who narrowed her eyes at me, giving me a once over. "What sort of clothes are those?" she asked loudly. "And that hair? How'd you get it like that?"

Everyone close by turned to stare. I was wearing plain blue jeans and a t-shirt, but my jacket was a bright purple fleece; it wasn't that different to what my classmates wore back home. But my clothes were new, different.

Even the Raturro girl raised her head to look at me. Her eyes met mine and a flicker of recognition went through me. Her big brown doe eyes blinked in the sun. Her ears perked up and turned towards me. Who was she? She cocked her head at an angle as if she were thinking the same thing.

I slipped my hand into my jeans pocket and grasped the little white button I had pulled off my stuffed animal.

"Mercy?" I whispered at the Raturro girl. She reminded me of the stuffed Mercy that sat on my bed, even her tattered dress was similar.

"Mercy?" I called out to her. The rat girl's eyes went wide in recognition and wonder. I inhaled sharply. "Mercy!"

My hand shot up. "One hundred," I shouted. Mercy didn't take her eyes off me.

"What're you doing?" asked Coyne, suddenly at my side trying to pull me away.

"One twenty-five" was called out from somewhere behind us.

"One fifty," I countered. "I need to save her," I whispered to Coyne.

"A Raturro?" Coyne scoffed. "We're supposed to keep a low profile. It's not safe here. Let's go." He tried to pull me away again, but I wouldn't budge.

"Two hundred," the voice from behind continued.

"What are you doing? We don't have any money," Coyne said.

"You didn't tell me the Raturro were slaves," I said.

"You never asked," he said, angry now. "C'mon."

"Two fifty," I shouted, raising my hand again. Suddenly the crowd hushed, and they were all staring at me, or more specifically, at my bracelet, which had slipped out from under my sleeve. Coyne pulled my hand down, but it was too late. There was a commotion in the crowd as they whispered and moved away from us.

The scar-faced man and his group of friends moved in on us, so I jumped up on the platform and ran to Mercy, who seemed just as stunned as I was. I raised my hand again, my bracelet shining in the sun.

"I'm Kyra Murch!" I shouted, suddenly brave. The crowd went completely quiet. Nobody moved.

Coyne looked aghast and mouthed, "What are you doing?"

I froze. I didn't have a plan. I just knew that it was Mercy, the real Mercy, and I had to save her. I stared out over the crowd of people—farmers, soldiers, and maybe even spies.

"I'm Kyra Murch," I repeated, stalling for time. "The Thane of Antiica, my father, has sent me. This Raturro belongs to me," I said as confidently as I could, glancing at Coyne. Hopefully he knew a way out of there, fast.

"What about the prophecy?" the scar-faced man shouted.

"Uh, the prophecy is a lie," I stammered, not really knowing what it was. "Our enemies started the story to scare us all, and it worked, didn't it?" I grinned as if it was a joke, and the crowd seemed to believe me. As they nodded and mumbled, I stuck my hand up in a royal wave, grabbed Mercy's furry arm, and pulled her off the platform. Coyne pushed through the crowd to join us.

"Hey, what about my money?" the old woman called after us.

"Send the bill to my father!" I shouted back at her. "Let's get out of here," I said as we rushed down the steps towards a nearby street.

I ushered Mercy towards Coyne, who glowered at her. "I'm not going anywhere with this rat."

Mercy reached out her small pinkish paws, soft and warm, and I took them in my hands, so big in comparison. "Is it really you, Kyra?" Mercy whispered.

"Mercy, you're real. I thought you were a stuffed mouse," I said.

"Oh, Kyra. That was a toy my mother made for you. So you would never forget us," she said, her big brown eyes brimming with tears. "And you didn't."

"I couldn't let them hurt you anymore," I said. We stood there for a few moments, my hands tightly grasping her paws.

"Are you coming, Kyra?" asked Coyne impatiently.

I had barely turned to answer him when there was a whistling sound in the air. Then an explosion rocked the ground and the dirt under my feet trembled and buckled.

People screamed. Mercy's paws were pulled from my hands by the force of the blast. We went flying to the ground and debris and dust from the explosion rained down upon us. Smoke filled the air and there was screaming and crying. I forced myself up off the ground and pulled Coyne up with me just as another blast rocked the market.

"The Raturro! Get your weapons," a man screamed behind us.

Mercy was still down on the ground, weak, her hands shackled. I reached for her.

"Leave her. The Raturro will save her," yelled Coyne above the commotion.

I gazed deep into Mercy's eyes. Coyne was right. Mercy was the enemy, but I couldn't help but feel that there was a reason for finding her.

Mercy cried weakly, "Ko-ru-ku."

"She's coming with us," I yelled above another blast.

"Run!" shouted Coyne, heading towards a narrow alley.

I grabbed Mercy's paws, pulled her to her feet, and we ran up the alley after Coyne, narrowly escaping the next round of artillery that rained down on the market. Mercy was weak and slow. I put an arm around her, supported her, felt the bony skeleton under her fur.

As we got to the middle of the long alleyway, I spied the rebel Raturro army up ahead blocking our passage. They had surrounded the town. There was no way out. A series of fortified wagons, pulled by huge menacing Raturro, sped by. Raturro stood in the back of the wagons, like centurions, dressed for battle in a hodgepodge of leather and canvas. Most wore dark leather vests and khaki pants, large rifles slung over their backs.

In the lead wagon, a tall, dominant Raturro stood surveying the scene. I flashed back to my vision. "Majellan," I stammered.

Mercy squeaked in fear.

The ferocious Raturro growled and revealed a mouthful of long, sharp teeth. He had lost part of one ear, and his fur was heavy, dark, and stood on end on top of his head like a Mohawk cut. He leered right at me. "It's the Murch! I want her!" Majellan barked, pointing a long sharp claw my way.

We quickly backed down the alley, frantically trying the doors and finally found one that was unlocked. "In here," I called to Coyne. We rushed inside a deserted bakery where the sweet aroma of fresh bread still hung in the air. There were some small black loaves and seed-speckled rolls on the counter. I grabbed a few and tossed them to Mercy who stared at me incredulously.

"What should I do with this?" she whispered.

"We'll take it with us," I said.

As Coyne barricaded the door with furniture, Mercy, still dazed by her escape, crumpled to the ground. She sat there on the flour-covered tiles, hugging the loaves of bread. "Take us where?" squeaked Mercy.

"Mercy, it's going to be okay." I told her. But she stared at me doubtfully.

"This was a bad idea. Now we're trapped," shouted Coyne.

I felt a spark in my brain. A buzz. I instantly knew I could summon the chimera and was excited by the prospect of seeing her again. I ran my hand over the wall. "Sandstone," I muttered as the information flashed through my mind. A common sedimentary rock, warm gold in colour, particles of quartz, silica, and calcium carbonate, a stone used for building and paving. I didn't know what it was for, but it seemed important.

"Chimera. Chimera I need your help. Where are you?" Then the stone was empty, no life in it. *"Chimera. Chimera!"*

A blast shook the building, dust and splintered rock fell on our heads. Mercy jumped and Coyne moaned in frustration.

"Chimera!! Answer me!" I shouted at the wall.

The door rattled as the Raturro tried to get inside. Coyne screamed, "I can't hold them any longer."

"It's not working," I shrieked as I slapped the wall. "Chimera!"

The second blast knocked Mercy back to her senses. She dropped the bread, scurried over to me and took my hand. Gazing deep into my eyes, she rubbed my bracelet with her soft pink paw. "Shhh, Ko-ru-ku. Shhh." Her soothing voice settled my nerves. I leaned against the wall again, felt the firm stone at my back. "Shhh, shhh…breathe. Shut out the noise. Listen to your heart."

A few deep breaths and the noise fell away. A warm, tingling sensation started under my bracelet, crept up my arm to my neck and head. My thoughts ebbed away, and the ring of fire returned. A shiver went up my spine. She was coming. The chimera was on her way.

An explosion of light hit the bakery and the chimera lit up the room. I struggled with the pain in my head. I was frightened and relieved at the same time. Where could she take us? I had no idea what orders to give her. Mercy's eyes sparkled and she smiled in amazement, then she confidently picked the bread up off the floor and filled her apron with it.

"Where to?" I asked Coyne, who was holding the door closed with all his might.

"South, to the Plains," said Coyne.

"No," countered Mercy authoritatively. "Deep Nestling. That's where we must go. We'll be safe there. It's my home."

"We can't trust the rat," he urged me. "She'll get us killed."

Something hit the door and the wood splintered inwards. Coyne went flying to the floor. A large clawed paw reached in through a gap in the door and scraped at the wood.

"Hurry! Majellan will kill us all!" squealed Mercy as I ran to Coyne and helped him up. I pulled him over to the chimera and hoped I could take them both with me. I wasn't sure where we should go. The Plains or Deep Nestling?

Mercy stared intently at me and simply said, "Ko-ru-ku."

"Let's go." I grabbed Mercy's paw and Coyne's hand, and the three of us jumped into the light.

CHAPTER NINE

"Kyra? Are you okay?" Coyne's voice faded in and out.

"You're supposed to hold your breath," squeaked Mercy.

"I did," I moaned. The pain in my head wasn't as bad this time, but it still hurt. I opened my eyes to see Coyne and Mercy's concerned faces staring down at me. "Did we make it through the wall?"

Mercy helped me sit up. We were in a small dim cave. Basalt. The most common of the volcanic rocks.

"So where are we now?" demanded Coyne. "And why did we bring this thing with us?" Coyne didn't even try to hide his disdain for Mercy. He moved to the mouth of the cave, eyes darting. Beyond him there was a misty, forested valley, divided by a black snaking river. Behind it was a vast snow-capped mountain range that seemed to stretch on forever.

"If you want the pain to stop, you must embrace the chimera," whispered Mercy, keeping one eye on Coyne.

"What does that even mean?" I asked.

"Once it controls you, you will control it," she said. "The chimera is ancient. You must do its bidding."

"How do you know that?" I asked her.

"I lived in the Reach for many years with your family, even after you left."

"Is this Deep Nestling?" I peered out at the rugged landscape.

"No, this is the Corvid Range," she said, her paw gesturing to the mountains. "Behind them is Deep Nestling and then Murch City. Don't worry, we are far from danger now."

"But we were closer to Murch City before, in Fuuto," I shouted. "The rebels have captured my mom. She's in Thane's Reach."

"The rebels have the queen?" Mercy squeaked.

I ran to the cave wall. "Chimera? Why did you bring us here?" I slammed my hand against it. "Chimera?"

Silence.

"How will I find Mom now?"

"Maybe there is a way," Mercy was thoughtful. "We could follow the river downstream and cross at the narrows, go through the Corvid Pass." Her claws gestured to a distant point. "It's a few days away, but we can always ask for passage over the mountains."

"Over the mountains?" I asked.

"Ask who?" demanded Coyne.

Mercy's big eyes blinked with surprise, "The Corvie, of course. They will give us passage."

"What're the Corvie?" I asked.

"Believe me, you don't want to meet the Corvie," warned Coyne. "Huge black birds. They eat human flesh. It's a delicacy in these parts. That's why the rebels will never expect an attack from behind these mountains. Nobody would be crazy enough to enter them."

"I will help you, Kyra. You have saved me from a life of slavery. The prophecy is true, Ko-ru-ku. I will go with you to Thane's Reach. There is always a way," she said proudly. The shackles on her paws couldn't dim her fighting spirit. Her eyes lit up as she schemed. "We only need a plan."

"Oh Mercy, thank you." I turned to Coyne. "Mercy knows the Reach. She can get us inside."

Coyne's laugh echoed through the cave. "I'm not going on some crazy rescue mission to a guarded castle in the middle of a vermin-infested city."

"But it's the Queen. If you helped rescue her, you'd be a hero in all of Murch City, in all of Antiica. My family would reward you. I'll make sure of it."

"I'm not hoping for riches or rewards, Kyra. I just want to get home," he said with a catch in his voice.

"Please, Coyne. Please help us." I pleaded.

Coyne stashed a loaf of bread in his long coat and went to the mouth of the cave. "I'm heading home," he pointed south. "It's only a few days walk from here. You can come with me, Kyra. It's safe there." The invitation didn't include Mercy, so I shook my head, no. "If you know what's good for you, you'll go back to your father." He started down the mountainside with a wary eye on the sky.

"Wait," I shouted. "Coyne, you can't just leave. At least hear what Mercy has to say."

"I don't listen to vermin," he shouted back.

"You said you would help me."

"You'll be fine with your new friend."

"But I just saved your life. You owe me," I yelled after him.

"Saved you first!"

"Did not! You're a coward, that's what you are," I called after him. He just kept on marching down the hill, easily navigating the steep terrain of rocks, scrub, and small trees. "Coyne," I whispered, fighting back tears. He'd been kind of a jerk, but I knew there was good in him too.

"We don't need him," Mercy huffed, jangling the chains on her wrists.

"Let me see that." I examined the shackles. Selecting a rock from a nearby pile, I bashed the chain. Whoever made them, had made them to last. As I pounded the chains I felt a sudden kinship with the rocks. Igneous. Metamorphic. Sedimentary. I could feel their power with every pounding movement I made. After many tries, the chain binding Mercy's paws together finally snapped open.

"I always knew you'd come back, Kyra," said Mercy as she threw her furry rat arms around me.

In that moment, I had a blur of thought, a memory. Mercy was a true friend, an ally, a sister even. With Mercy's alter ego, the stuffed Mercy in my arms, we would play for hours together. "I remember now," I said. "We had tea parties and played games. We were friends."

"Yes, Kyra. Oh, yes! Where have you been? When you and the Queen disappeared, we feared you were dead."

"I've been on another world, Mercy." Mercy blinked rapidly and I wasn't sure if she believed me or not.

"That is possible," she said. "Yes, it would be the only place Majellan couldn't find you. The Queen was very shrewd to find such a place."

"It's called Earth, and there are no Raturro there, just humans. Well, until a few days ago."

"Start a fire," she instructed. "I will find us some better food than that manure." She pointed at the bread. Then she dashed off towards the river before I could to stop her.

Fire. How was I supposed to make a fire? My bracelet glinted as it caught the sunlight. "Help me, Chimera," I pleaded with the wall. I rubbed my bracelet like Mercy had shown me while I thought of the chimera.

No reply.

I'd have to make one myself. I scoured the area outside of the cave for twigs and some bigger bits of wood. It took a while to find flint, as the database in my head identified every stone I picked up. I finally found a tiny shard. Sitting on the cave floor, I tried to spark it but the wood refused to light. I was glad that Mercy couldn't see me. Or Coyne, he'd only scoff at me and call me princess.

Holding the shard tightly in my fist, I concentrated. I envisioned fire in my mind's eye, and then the stone in my hand became warm. As it got hotter and hotter, I opened my fist and dropped the rock into the wood. The flint glowed like an ember and caused the wood to ignite. Finally, the fire was lit. I stared at my hand, amazed that I could even do something like that.

Mercy was soaking wet as she clamored back up the rocky hill on two legs, proudly carrying two large, fierce, spiky orange fish in her apron. She was happy to see the fire. With her sharp claws, Mercy expertly cut the flesh off the bone, speared hunks of creamy orange fish onto sticks and set them into the fire. The aroma of the cooking fish filled the cave as we waited.

"Mercy, did you know someone named Shale?

"Shale is my fifth uncle by marriage, why?"

"He came to find me on Earth," I said and I wondered how to tell her the rest.

"I heard that Shale left the Nestling because he wanted to find a way to stop the war. Then he joined the rebels. I'm sure he was only obeying orders from Majellan. I know he would never harm you, Kyra."

"He didn't. He tried to warn me, save me, but the chimera came and took him away."

A look of alarm flashed in Mercy's eyes. I wasn't sure if I should tell her the rest, so we sat and stared at the fire. Silent.

When the fish was cooked, I stuffed it inside the bread and made sloppy sandwiches. I watched Mercy politely turn the sandwich over in her paw, then hand it back to me. She snatched up the discarded fish heads instead and her sharp teeth effortlessly crunched through the fish skulls.

"Is there really a prophecy about me?"

Mercy nodded, thoroughly enjoying the fish, "The Last Murch will free the Raturro. You have freed me, Ko-ru-ku. You can free us all."

"I don't know about that. Shale called me Ko-ru-ku. What does it mean?"

"Ko-ru-ku is the name the Raturro gave you. It means 'a powerful child will come.' Your birth was celebrated amongst all Raturro because we find hope in the youngest—the purest. Some of the Nestlings support Majellan, but some do not feel the same way about the war and fear Majellan. Deep Nestling Raturro want to live in peace, so we avoid Thane's Reach and everything it now stands for."

"But why did Majellan start the war in the first place?"

"Oh, Majellan never started the war. It was your father."

"What?"

"What has he told you about the Raturro? About the rebellion?"

"Nothing. Absolutely nothing."

"Your father enslaved the Raturro, Kyra. That is why there is a rebellion. That is why Majellan fights back. The Nestlings fear Majellan because…" she hesitated, unsure if she should go on. "Well, because he has become just as bad as your father. There are rumours he's tortured Raturro who don't do his bidding."

I sat, horrified, knowing it was true. "Mercy, I have something to tell you about Shale."

As we silently made camp for the night, I could see Mercy was upset about Shale. How could Dad have done this? I would be nothing like him.

"Ko-ru-ku," I whispered to the fire. It felt like my real name. Perhaps I was never a Kyra at all.

When I awoke, it was dark outside, the sun a sliver of light rising on the horizon, the brilliant green Moons of Juris fading above it. Mercy was still in the same spot but her ears twitched with danger. "Someone's coming," she warned.

Mercy peered down the hill and in the early morning gloom I could see a figure.

"It's only the coward."

"Coyne!" I grinned, surprised to see him back so quickly. He must've camped nearby and probably realized how badly he'd behaved and was coming back to apologize. I didn't care about apologies. I was just happy to see him. But as he closed in on us, it became obvious that there was something terribly wrong.

"Put out the fire," he called, his face in a fearful grimace.

I kicked dirt on it as Coyne ran into the cave, out of breath.

"The rebels are coming," he panted. "The patrol caught my scent."

"Then why come back here?" Mercy cried. "You've led them to us."

"I had to warn you," he raised his voice. "You can see your fire for leagues."

"How long before they're here?" I asked.

"They're right behind me," said Coyne.

I approached the wall where the chimera had brought us through, took a deep breath. "Chimera." I rubbed my bracelet frantically. "Chimera, please!"

"Take us to Deep Nestling," Mercy said. "They will protect you."

"The Plains are safer," said Coyne.

"Look, I don't care where the chimera takes us, but I know that if we find my mom, she can help us," I said. "Mercy, do you know how to make the chimera take us into Murch City?" She shook her head, no.

"It would not be safe to enter the city without a plan, Kyra," she said worriedly. The City Raturro answer only to Majellan."

Coyne, who had moved to the mouth of the cave to stand guard, turned to me. "Look, over there." My eyes followed his gaze and I saw the telltale dust cloud behind the rebels' swift moving wagons. They wouldn't be able to drive up the hill, but if they were as quick as Mercy was when she dashed to the river, it wouldn't take them long.

"If I'm caught with you, they'll say I'm a traitor. They'll skin me alive." She trembled.

Chimera, we need to leave here. We need to get out of here.

"We'll have to get to the other side of the river at least," said Mercy. "Or further into the Corvid Range. Anywhere but here."

The chimera was quiet. I rubbed my bracelet again. Nothing.

"The wagon's stopped," said Coyne.

Mercy ran to him and gazed down the mountain.

"What are our chances?" Coyne asked her.

"The chimera is our only hope." Mercy ran to me. "You have access to so much power, Kyra. Do you know that?"

"What do you mean?"

"How long have you been one with the chimera?"

"A few days?"

Mercy inhaled sharply, "This is not good. It takes years to master it. Oh." Her eye went back to the cave mouth.

"Fire," I said. "I can make fire. That will stop them, won't it?"

Mercy eyed the ashes of the fire skeptically.

"Go, gather whatever wood you can carry and pile it up outside the cave. We need fuel," I ordered her. "You too, Coyne."

I reached into the ashes and found the small piece of flint. Could this little rock really help us, I wondered. I ran to the mouth of the cave and sat down, sensing the depth of the mountain below me. For a moment I watched as Mercy and Coyne worked together to carry a large log and place it on the growing pile of wood. This had to work. It was our only chance.

I glanced down the hill and could see a group of small grey figures running up the hill on all fours. "They're here!" I called, and Coyne and Mercy scrambled back up.

I closed my eyes and held the stone in my fist. *Cryptocrystalline, mineral quartz. Flint.*

Fire. I thought. *Fire!*

A vision of flames erupted in my head. A sudden warmth bloomed in my hand. I held onto it, let it grow hotter. It burned into my palm, sizzled my fingers, and snaked up my arm. I opened my eyes to find my hand awash with a blue glow. I dropped the flint onto the pile of wood and it exploded into flames.

In my peripheral vision I could see half a dozen huge Raturro only a hundred meters away.

"It's not enough," whispered Mercy behind me.

"Fire!" I shouted again. A strange desire burned inside of me as I felt the chimera creep inside of my head. She took hold of me and the stream of flames from my hand grew in intensity. The flames moved away from the burning wood and spewed its heat along the strand of trees effectively creating a wall of fire between the Raturro and the cave.

I fought a growing urge to incinerate the Raturro who ran back and forth in front of the raging flames looking for a break in the heat, unsure how to proceed but bursting with the need to capture us.

Suddenly I felt Mercy's soft paws around my shoulders. "Enough, Kyra. Stop." The fiery blaze in front of us almost blinded me. Then I realized the chimera was lit up on the wall behind us.

Coyne was quickly by my side and he and Mercy grabbed my arms. I saw the fear in his eyes. Was he afraid of the Raturro or me?

The chimera was back in my head. "We need to cross the river," I thought through the pain. "Take us to Murch City. Take us to my mother."

We can only take you to safety.

"Come on, there must be some way. Ko-ru-ku?"

We cannot take you into danger—

"Okay!" I exclaimed, frustrated. "Just take us away from here."

We all took a deep breath and jumped into the chimera, not knowing where we would end up.

CHAPTER TEN

"The river," shouted Mercy as we emerged from a sheer cliff face. The slippery scree below our feet had us stumbling and careening towards a dark forest. Mercy scrambled ahead of us, doubling back when she realized Coyne was still picking me up off the rocks.

"What happens when we get to the river?" I asked, reeling from travel through the chimera.

"We'll have to cross it, of course," Mercy replied, her nose hungrily sniffing the air. She pointed to a not-so-distant peak behind us and we could see the trees I had set on fire. I had hoped the chimera would take us further away from danger. It was my fault; I didn't know how to work it.

"The smoke might mask our scent for a while, but there are other Raturro in this forest." She sniffed again. "Oh, so many. This way."

Coyne hesitated a moment before following her, worry etched on his face. "What is it?" I asked.

"Nothing," he said.

"We have to follow her. She's the only one who knows the way."

He didn't look too sure. The hatred in this world had surprised me in so many ways. I was beginning to understand his animosity towards Mercy and the Raturro; he'd been taught to hate them, been forced to fight them. I felt the hatred too. Majellan was ferocious and the fact he had captured Mom was making me despise him too.

"Kyra?"

The ache in my head was back, pounding like a drum.

"You're bleeding." He touched my ear and held up his fingers to show me.

"Hurry!" shouted Mercy, far ahead of us. She scrambled over the rocks towards the thick dark forest between us and the river.

"I'm okay," I lied and wiped the blood away with my sleeve. I had to keep going. I pushed Coyne ahead of me and stumbled behind him trying to keep up.

Mercy set a grueling pace and Coyne easily kept up with her, but my chest was tight with pain as we ran through the woods. Setting the fire and then coming through the chimera had taken a terrible toll on me. My head ached, and I was shivering uncontrollably but sweaty too. When we paused to get our bearings, I bent over, panting, my mouth already parched. The sun was rising behind us but it was still night in the forest, the tall, black leaved trees like dark sentinels standing in our way.

Running ahead of Coyne, I pushed myself faster, hoping the river would be shallow enough to wade through. Swimming was not my best sport, and I hated getting water in my nose and ears. Soon, Coyne passed me on the path, and I ran harder, desperate to keep up.

We emerged into a clearing and Mercy's paw was in the air signaling us to stop. Her nose twitched and her ears swiveled back and forth on high alert. Then her ears froze. Something was in the woods.

We crept away, hoping to circle around through the forest and avoid what was surely a Raturro patrol. As we ran, we tried not to make any noise but the forest floor was littered with dry twigs that snapped on contact. Mercy stopped us again and we ducked down behind a fallen tree.

I should've had the chimera take us back to the Armory, to safety, but I had a feeling it wasn't the best place for Mercy. And then no one would be helping Mom. She would be a prisoner forever. I wondered what Dad was doing—would he really let that happen? Would he be looking for me? I was still angry with him. If he could send the chimera to protect me, why couldn't he come visit himself? I always wondered why he missed so many birthdays, but now I knew. He cared more about fighting this war and killing Raturro than me and Mom.

Mercy was on all fours creeping away from the safety of the log. She scratched the bark on a tree, and then rubbed her fur against it, leaving her scent on the trees to confuse the Raturro. She disappeared under some shrubs and after what seemed like a long, long time, she crept up behind us and quietly ushered us in a new direction. The sound of the Raturro yelping and angrily crashing through the wood reached us and drove us onward.

"There's no way we can do this." Coyne kicked a rock into the river. "The current's too fast." Up close, the river was much wider, a mass of swirling eddies and undercurrents. Even the strongest swimmer would have a hard time reaching the other side. He attempted to pick up a thin log that was strewn on the rocky shore, but it was too heavy. "Maybe we could lash some of these together."

"There's no time," said Mercy, snout in the air. "The wind has carried our scent upstream. They could be here at any moment."

Coyne fidgeted. "There's got to be another way," he said.

"You can't swim?" I asked, incredulous.

"I'm from the Plains. We don't need to swim there."

Mercy scoffed. "We have a saying: You are either the stone or the wood. You must decide."

"What's that supposed to mean?" Coyne asked.

"Sink or swim." I sighed. This was not good.

"Get into the water," Mercy ordered. "I will help you across, human. Unless you want to stay and take your chances with the rebels?" She ventured into the raging torrent.

"How do I know you won't let me drown?" Coyne called after her.

"Please, Coyne, just try," I interrupted before Mercy could answer. I glanced back at the forest expecting to be ambushed at any moment, but Coyne wouldn't budge. "Fine. Take your chances with the rebels," I said and waded into the roiling current. The rocks were slippery. I quickly lost my footing and fell into the freezing water with a scream.

Coyne angrily removed his heavy coat and tied it around his waist, but he stopped at the water's edge, terrified to go further. Mercy bobbed in the water behind us, her strong tail already fighting the current.

"You can do it," I whispered to Coyne. He grimaced and waded towards Mercy, whose fearful eyes darted up and down the shoreline. Coyne and I submerged ourselves up to our necks. "Ready?" He looked as if I'd given him a death sentence.

Mercy squeaked out an alarm. A lone Raturro scout had emerged from the woods further upstream and caught our scent. Mercy disappeared under the dark water and reappeared beside Coyne. Grabbing the scruff of his neck, she pulled him into the raging water.

"Keep your head above water and kick your legs as hard as you can," I shouted over the roar of the water and dove after them.

The fast moving current quickly pulled us downstream away from the lone Raturro, who galloped along the rocky beach towards us. My clothes were heavy with water and it grew harder to propel myself forward. Soon my arms and legs felt sluggish, and I'd swallowed so much water that I felt sick.

Mercy was a strong swimmer and kept Coyne, a look of terror on his face, from sinking. Behind us, more Raturro emerged from the forest and ran along the beach, but they weren't pursuing us into the river. Yet.

"Kyra!" Mercy called over the roar of the river. She pointed ahead to a series of wild rapids in our path. Beyond was a telltale cloud of vapor reaching for the sky. A waterfall.

Back onshore, the pack of Raturro were running on all fours alongside the river keeping pace. I hoped the threat of the waterfall would keep them from following us.

A log floated nearby and I swam towards it hoping Mercy would follow. She saw it too and expertly swam past me, a frantic Coyne in tow. Grabbing a hold of the log, Mercy steadied Coyne as he wrapped his arms around it.

We were soon in the rapids and then suddenly I was underwater. The raging river had me in its grasp. I couldn't breathe. I fought, not knowing which way was up. In a moment of despair, I let the current carry me to what I thought was certain doom. Then miraculously my head was above water and Mercy was pulling me up by the hair. She grabbed my arm and pulled me towards the shore.

"Coyne?" I sputtered. He was still hanging onto the log and heading straight for the falls.

"I can only save one. It must be you," shouted Mercy above the fury of the rapids that now tossed us.

"No, Mercy!" If something happened to him, it would be my fault. He trusted me. The rapids pushed us straight at a huge rock, then, at the last second, pulled us apart. I seized the opportunity to swim downstream towards Coyne.

"Kyra!" she called after me but I had to reach Coyne. He was in danger because of me and I wasn't going to let him die. The rapids were a maze of rocks, and I rode the swift water further and further downstream towards the falls. I hoped Coyne, clinging to the log and barely conscious, could hang on long enough.

"Coyne!" My fingers slipped on the slimy log but latched onto a submerged branch. I inched closer. "Coyne!"

When he finally lifted his head, the roar around us was deafening. We were only a hundred meters from certain death. "Let go!" I screamed. In a moment of utmost trust, he let go of the log. I lunged for him and we both went under. It seemed like forever until we bobbed up to the surface. Coyne wasn't moving anymore. I couldn't lift his head out of the water and fight the current at the same time. Coyne was drowning. I felt so powerless, so afraid. The river was stronger than all of us.

"No!" I screamed as the current yanked him from me and pulled him under.

Ahead of me, Mercy's head broke the surface and she had Coyne in her grasp. With near super strength, she caught my hand and steered us all to the opposite shore with only moments to spare.

I pressed down hard on Coyne's chest with my hands. I'd only seen CPR done on TV shows, and I had no idea if I could bring him back to life. One, two, three. I pressed again. One, two, three. I leaned my head on his chest. His heart was beating—that was a good sign. But he wasn't breathing. There was only one thing I could think to do: I placed my lips on his and forced a blast of hot air into his lungs.

I barely even had time to think how gross it was that I was sort of kissing a boy when he wheezed. His eyes opened and I found Coyne's face close to mine for what seemed an endless moment. He held my gaze and I could see he was amazed to be alive. I was amazed any of us were still alive. Then he turned over and retched a stomachful of river water onto the rocky beach. I'd never been so thankful in my life. He was okay.

"Ko-ru-ku?" Mercy whispered. I glanced from one soaking friend to the other and nodded I was fine.

We were on the precipice of the waterfall only steps from where it plummeted hundreds of meters down to the craggy rocks below. A heavy mist shielded the far shore, and I had no idea whether the Raturro could see us or would emerge from the water at any moment. Mercy's nose twitched in the air. We had to keep moving.

We lifted Coyne to his feet, but his legs buckled. Even though I was exhausted, I heaved his arm over my shoulder to support his weight. Mercy took his other arm and we half-dragged him along the rocky shore. Soaked, exhausted, and lost, we slipped into the shadowy forest and hoped the rebels would think we had perished in the mighty river.

CHAPTER ELEVEN

"What was that river called, Mercy? Does it have a name?" It would be forever etched in my memory, even if it was nameless.

"The Soulcatcher," she whispered as we supported Coyne between us and moved deeper into the thick forest, stumbling over tree roots. It was slow going. We were guided by Mercy's super-sensitive nose scouting for patrols up ahead.

Still, we would have to risk making a fire or Coyne would freeze. I worried about hypothermia as he shivered against me, teeth chattering. It felt like we had walked for hours. With every twig snap, I imagined the Raturro jumping out of the dark trees and slicing us with their razor sharp claws.

Mercy found us a safe clearing and began gathering kindling while I pulled Coyne out of his damp coat. Soon we were warm and our clothes gave off steam as they dried. Coyne barely uttered a word for the rest of the day.

Nightfall came and the last thing I remember was Mercy reassuring me, "No Raturro have passed this way in a very long time."

"Coyne?" I whispered, waking the next morning in a panic. "Mercy?"

All I could hear was birdsong. No roaring river. The campfire was cold. Only little blue windows of sky above me penetrated the dark, shadowy forest all around me. When I tried to stand a sharp pain shot through my right ankle. I sat back down hard.

I fumbled in my damp jacket pocket for the photograph sure that the river had ruined it. It was all I had left of my family. I held it up to a patch of sunlight and the photo gleamed in the light. Mom, Dad and I still stood and smiled under the tree. How had it survived the river? How had I survived that river?

Looking closer at the paper's waxy protective coating, a shimmer caught my eye—a series of lines, silvery-blue in colour, forming a pattern in a floating hologram. Curious. I tucked it safely back in my pocket.

My ankle throbbed so I pulled off my battered running shoe. It was badly bruised. What if it was broken? There were no hospitals out here.

"Put your shoe back on," Mercy said, startling me. "Your foot will swell up and then you'll never get it back on."

"Where'd Coyne go?" As I retied my shoe, my shoulders and arms ached.

"The human survived. He's looking for food, but he doesn't get very far before coming back to check on you. You've made quite an impression on him. I didn't think humans from the Plains were capable of feelings."

"Here. It's not much." She pulled a handful of berries out of her apron pocket. "But I'm sure we'll find more later." Black and seedy, like raspberries, they were sticky sweet and delicious. I licked the juice off my fingers.

"Where are we?"

"We're far enough away from the rebels that they won't pick up our trail," she said wearily. "It doesn't look like they wanted you badly enough to cross the Soulcatcher and venture into Corvie territory."

I gazed up at the sky half-expecting the great birds to be watching us, ready to swoop down at any moment. "They'll help us get to Murch City?"

"They'll wait until we're out in the open. That's good for us. We can gather our strength and be prepared for our meeting."

"How do you prepare for giant, flesh-eating birds?" Coyne slipped through the stand of trees.

"Those who have met the Corvie were very respectful to them and survived," said Mercy.

"How?" I asked.

"Like this. Prostrate." Mercy bowed down, nose to ground.

"Right. Just lie there and let them feed off the buffet. Do they even eat rats like you?" said Coyne.

How could he say that after Mercy had helped carry him through the forest to safety? Or did he remember when Mercy chose to save me and not him?

"It doesn't matter to the Corvie. They'll eat anything," Mercy said, her anger showing. Then she softened and turned to me. "What matters is your heart. If it's true, they'll listen to you."

"Before or after they rip it out of her chest?" Coyne added.

"You could always go back the way we came," I said to him. He shuddered.

Mercy ignored him to focus on fashioning a tree bough into a crutch for me.

"Everything was fine until we met that rat," he said, under his breath as he bent down for his coat. "Now, we're being chased by the rebels and searching for giant birds that could eat us whole for breakfast."

"Look, I'm just as mad about the whole rebel thing as you are, but it's not my fault there's a war. It's not any of our faults. And if you two don't stop whatever fight you're having, I'll just go by myself to find my mom."

Coyne and Mercy stared at each other. We were all scared, tired, and hungry. The Soulcatcher had taken a heavy toll on us.

Mercy was the first to bend and she raised her paws in mock surrender, "We must go." She handed me the crutch and the three of us started our journey through the forest. It was slow going over the uneven forest floor. Though it was relatively clear from scrub and rocks, the tree roots sat like giant gnarled hands and some of the fingers were big enough to walk under. I had to move carefully to avoid banging my ankle again. Mercy and Coyne would hop from root to root but I had to walk around. Fortunately, my ankle seemed to improve as my muscles warmed up.

Soon we came to a small rivulet of water and stopped to gulp it down. Every swallow reminded me of choking for air underwater, of nearly drowning.

"How far until we find these big birds?" asked Coyne.

"I don't know. The next valley?" replied Mercy. "Perhaps we'll find some more food." Coyne nodded, clearly happy at the thought of a meal.

I was starving again. We all were, but there was nothing for miles, just the towering dark trees. I felt a bit spooked.

Despite Mercy scouting ahead and behind us, I felt as if we were being watched. Tiny white birds with sharp red beaks kept us company on our journey and after a long while I was sure it was the same bird following me, watching me.

"Sorry, but I need another break," I said.

"I'll scout ahead," said Mercy impatiently.

"No, wait. Tell me more about the chimera."

"Kyra," she started, with an odd look towards Coyne. "I'm sure your father wouldn't want you discussing it in public."

"Public?" laughed Coyne.

"Coyne is my friend and—"

"Humans can't be trusted," she said, marching away down the trail.

"But I'm a human!" I protested.

"You are Ko-ru-ku. The chosen one," she corrected as she scampered away.

"I wouldn't pay her any mind. The Raturro are known for their bluntness. If she wants to tell you something, she will. But you can't believe a thing those rats say, especially about that crazy prophecy."

"If Mercy says there's a prophecy about me, I believe her." Truth is, I didn't know if I wanted to be the subject of a prophecy or a part of the royal family. Just because it exists, doesn't mean it would come true. Yes, it was kind of cool to have a monster at my beck and call, but for the rest of my life? I would just give the bracelet back to Mom, if I could find her—when I found her.

"C'mon," Coyne said as he helped me up and followed Mercy deeper into the woods.

"Did you kill any Raturro in the war?" I asked Coyne.

Coyne jumped over a fallen log. "Soldiers don't discuss their kills."

"Oh." I glanced at him sideways as I slid over the log—was he really a killer? I thought back to the moment on the beach when my lips were on his. It was gross at the time, but since then I'd been thinking about it. His lips were so soft.

"Actually, I was never in any of the big battles," he said, interrupting my thoughts. "I was a munitions apprentice, fixed things mostly."

I sighed in relief. He'd never killed any Raturro. I would hate him if he did.

"Back home I'm pretty handy with the farm machinery, had to be since my dad was killed in the war."

"Oh, no! The Raturro killed your father?" I asked.

He nodded solemnly. "I went to the war because I thought I could help do something right, but it didn't work out that way."

"Mercy said my dad started the war."

Coyne held back a heavy branch so I could pass. "You'd get a different answer from everyone you asked. Some people say it was something personal between Majellan and the Thane."

"Personal? How?"

"They were friends once. Buddies. They went to school together."

"What? That's crazy." I almost fell over a tree root and Coyne grabbed my arm to steady me.

"You didn't know?" he asked.

"No, Dad never really talked about his childhood." I didn't mention that I'd hardly seen Dad in years, or that my family history was all but unknown to me.

"I've been trying to get home since before I met you. My term in the army was over. It was expected that I'd re-enlist immediately, but I said no. My commander wasn't happy about that, but she really couldn't stop me. What was I supposed to do? My mom and my sisters can't bring in the harvest all by themselves, and I miss them," his voice softened and he suddenly looked much younger. Just a boy.

"I'm sorry I took you out of your way," I said.

"Never thought I'd meet a princess," he teased, lightening the mood.

"Don't call me that." I went to punch him in the arm, but he ducked and I got him square on the face.

"Ow!"

"I'm so sorry, Coyne."

"You're always trying to beat me up, princess."

Instinctively I reached out to touch his face. His hand met mine for a moment and I felt my face heat up.

"Gotcha," he said, smiling warmly. He let go of my hand and we stood in awkward silence. He'd been so angry when I first met him. Lonely, maybe. Like me.

As we continued on, Coyne pointed to a bright spot through the trees. "Look!"

The trees thinned out and we were soon on the edge of a lush green valley nestled between the tallest of mountains. Star-shaped yellow flowers dotted a meadow. The air was warm and sweet, but something was wrong with the picture. That uneasy feeling crept over me again—like I was being watched. The little bird had disappeared, and I didn't hear any other birds or even see any in the sky.

"It's so quiet. Is that a pond down there?" I called to Mercy, who was searching along the tree line. She sensed it too. Something was off.

"Perhaps we should wait." Mercy sniffed the air nervously. "I can't quite…I don't recognize…."

Coyne pointed to a large berry bush at the edge of the meadow. "Kyra, over here." He ran to pull the black fruit off the spiky branches.

"Mercy, look!" I called, but she remained focused on the sky.

As we wolfed down a few handfuls of the sweet fruit, Coyne said, "My mom makes a berry pie like no other. I hope you can meet her someday." The sun dappled through the trees enhancing the gold flecks in his eyes.

I gazed into his deep eyes and was sorely tempted. I was on a mission to find Mom, but part of me wanted to run away and never see a Raturro again. I dug my crutch into the ground.

"Sure. Who doesn't love pie?" I glanced over at Mercy, then up. Nothing.

Coyne shuffled over to another berry bush leaving me in the cool shade, alone.

"It looks okay to me," I said.

"Yeah, c'mon. I'm ravenous," Coyne said.

I should have listened to that tiny voice in my head, but my hunger was louder.

Finally, Mercy shrugged. "Let's head for the pond, but stay hidden in the shadows."

Coyne rubbed his hands together. "I'm thinking fish for lunch?"

"Race ya!" I said, limping through open meadow. He matched my slow pace.

"Oh, c'mon. It's hardly a race," he said.

"Kyra, no, stick to the trees!" Mercy called after us.

"It's quicker this way," I called back.

"Wait, Kyra!" Mercy quickly caught up and we bolted through the long grass towards the pond at the bottom of the hill. Throwing my crutch aside, I was so happy to be out of the darkness of the forest, I barely felt any pain.

"C'mon, slowpoke," said Coyne, now ahead of me.

But Mercy let out a gasp of worry.

The land of Antiica, strange as it was, was beautiful on a sunny day. I felt relaxed, happy. Until immense bird talons clamped around my body and silently lifted me off the ground.

CHAPTER TWELVE

A bitter wind howled in my face and I could barely catch my breath as the ground shrank beneath me. Mercy and Coyne were nowhere to be seen in the sunny meadow below. My eyes darted around, trying to find them. Above me, a giant shadowy creature pumped its wings faster and faster. Higher and higher. The Corvie. I was helpless in the immense bird's grasp and could only imagine plummeting to my death if it let me go. Panicked, I grabbed its gigantic claw and held on tight. The wrinkled black flesh was surprisingly soft and warm.

Soon we rose above the snowy mountains and the air around me grew cold. In a matter of minutes, we had flown far over the vast mountain range and were headed for the highest snow-covered peak. My heart thudded in my chest. The Corvie could get us closer to Murch and Mom, but they could also gulp us down whole. At least we'd be safe from the Raturro, but what new trouble would we find?

Before I knew it, the huge bird hovered over a rocky outcrop. It loosened its grasp, gently setting me down on a smooth rock shelf carved out of glossy black obsidian. The shelf was worn from years of wind and snow, and it was bitter cold. The bird steadied me as I got my footing and then rose into the sky, its black wings became iridescent in the sun before disappearing into a cloud. Two more birds appeared out of the clouds and set Mercy and Coyne on the ledge. We instinctively grabbed onto each other as a huge gust of freezing wind came around the mountain and threatened to knock us over. Coyne's strong hand gripped my arm and Mercy's pink tail wrapped tightly around my leg.

"Now what?" I yelled over the howling wind, still trembling from the wildest ride of my life.

"This is good. This is very good," Mercy shouted back as the wind carried our voices away.

"Good? How can you possibly say this is—" Coyne stopped mid-sentence and I could see from his face that something had landed behind me. His grip on my arm tightened. The air was suddenly still and much warmer. The Corvie had stopped the wind.

"Get down!" Mercy pulled us both to our knees and then we were facedown on the hard rock. Prostrate.

"You never said these birds would be taking us for a ride!" Coyne shouted at Mercy.

"I never said they wouldn't," Mercy replied.

"What do we do now?" I asked.

"Treat them with utmost respect and do exactly as I say," she whispered as our faces met the cold rock. Seeing the look of worry on Coyne's face, I gripped his hand so hard I was sure I drew blood. Not a good thing when you're surrounded by huge flesh-eating creatures.

"RAWK!" The Corvie behind me let out a raucous call. It was followed by another. Then another. The giant birds had silently descended and created a circle around us. Peeking under my shoulder, I could make out a forest of black bird legs as thick as trees.

"RAWK!"

It was Mercy who moved first. In a slow, fluid movement she sat up but kept her head bowed. "Great Corvie Master, take pity on the weak and foolish who have bothered you today," she said. She was playing a role in some expected ritual, hopefully not a sacrificial one.

"RAWK. RAWK!" All the Corvie answered at once in an angry cacophony.

"I am Merkaydees Talayna Raturro of Deep Nestling. My mother was Pippamin Talayna Raturro, her mother was Jemmant Pippamin Talayna Raturro. Our family has lived in Deep Nestling since the stars first appeared in the sky, since the lost sisters of Juris found each other. Great Corvie Master, we need passage across the mountains. Only the Corvie can show us the way."

Mercy pressed her snout back down. Jabbing a sharp claw into Coyne's side, she whispered, "Get up slowly and repeat what I said—exactly."

Coyne fought for air. It was either nerves or the fact we were up so high. I could feel it too. The air was definitely thinner. Coyne kept his head bowed low. "Er, uh, Great Corvie Master, take pity on the weak and foolish who have bothered you today. I am Coyne Macken Thresh of the Great Plains. My father was Islaw Rood Thresh and my mother is Teelda Macken Thresh."

At the mention of the Thresh name, Mercy shot him a look of pure hatred.

"Our family has lived in Abbassiniboyne since—" he hesitated, "since the Stone Wars and we were given the land by the Thane. Great Corvie Master, we need passage across the mountains. Only the Corvie can show us the way."

Coyne prostrated himself again. Mercy nudged me hard. It was my turn.

"G-great Corvie Master, take pity on the weak and foolish who have bothered you today. I'm—I'm Kyra Murch and—"

RAWK! RAWK! The birds erupted into a murderous cackle.

I jumped up to my feet and craned my neck at the six giant black ravens encircling us. A dozen keen black eyes stared back. Suddenly, a huge black beak hammered the ground in front of me. Then I was face-to-face with a beady black eye examining me. I could see my small, warped reflection in its pupil.

"RAWK!" There was silence all around us. "What is your providence?" He spoke in a deep ancient voice.

"Providence?" I sputtered, shocked that the bird could speak.

Mercy whispered, "Family."

"I am the last Murch. My family—" I stopped. I didn't know who I was. "My father is Jaagar Murch, the Thane. My mother is Aerikka Murch, she's the queen." Another large beak crashed down on the rock. A beady eye scanned me.

"Uh," I continued, "Mom's been captured by the rebels and I have to save her. My dad's too busy with his stupid war. He didn't even remember my birthday!"

Another beak struck the ground.

"I know that sounds selfish, but, you see, I've only been on Antiica a few days. I came from Earth. Do you know what Earth is? It's far from here. And then there's the prophecy. I just want to rescue Mom and go home. She's in Murch City. Can you take us there?"

They didn't answer.

"Can you?" Words and thoughts whirled inside of my head until one rose to the top. "Ko-ru-ku?"

The birds spread their wings like a giant black velvet curtain around us. Beaks in the air, they sang in unison, "Ko-ru-ku! Ko-ru-ku! Ko-ru-ku!"

"Ko-ru-ku, little one." The leader watched me closely. "Your name has been in the wind since your destiny was written so long ago. We have watched for your arrival and will sing of it for time to come. Your heart is pure. You are welcome in our nest. We shall do your bidding. RAWK. I am Eebon, father of the Corvie."

"Eebon. I'm happy to meet you." A surge of warmth ran through me and on impulse I wrapped my arms around the Corvie's large beak. Mercy squeaked in terror but Eebon just chortled.

"And my friends are happy to meet you too." I let go.

Behind me, Coyne and Mercy slowly stood. Mercy grabbed hold of my arm, and Coyne nudged close to my shoulder.

"Only the brave leave the Corvie nest," squawked Eebon. "Not all your hearts are pure."

"I don't understand. We've trekked through the mountains to find you, Eebon. We braved the Soulcatcher, and the rebels chased us—"

"We've been watching you, little one. We cannot give safe passage to all of you. Only the pure of heart—"

"We are pure of heart!" I insisted.

The Corvie rawked and cawed.

Eebon spoke again, gently. "One of you does not leave the nest. You must choose which one."

"You have to let us all go. Please!"

But there was only silence. I turned to my friends. Mercy seemed downtrodden and Coyne, guilty. How was I supposed to pick one of my friends? Coyne had helped me instead of going home to his family. Yes, he had run off at one point, but only because of the way he felt about the Raturro. He hated them, but hatred is taught. I felt like I'd known Mercy forever. How could I leave her to be a captive again, or worse?

"Here, take this. Isn't it pretty?" I pulled off my bracelet and held it up to a sunbeam so it shimmered. On Earth, ravens liked shiny things.

"RAWK!"

"You can keep it in exchange for my friends' freedom. I can't leave either of them behind."

"No, Kyra," whispered Mercy. "You mustn't leave the bracelet." She was right. I had promised Mom I would never take it off. I needed it to find her and to contact the chimera. But I gave the bracelet to Eebon, who took it in his beak a moment then secured it on one of his claws like a ring.

"You value your friends, Ko-ru-ku," Eebon said. I nodded. They were all I had.

"Bring me what the Corvie seek every day and your bracelet shall be returned. If you do not, then you will live in our nest for eternity," Eebon said.

I stared into his big black eye, mesmerized, and nodded in a solemn promise that I didn't yet understand. Pulling away from Eebon's gaze I took one last look at the bracelet. It didn't look so shiny anymore. In that instant, the wind whipped us as the Corvie lifted their protective wings.

Suddenly Mercy was surrounded by the great Corvie claws and pulled away from us. She disappeared into the clouds and was gone. Next, Coyne was grabbed by one of the birds and swept up into the clouds. A warm gust of wind was all I felt as a bird wrapped its talons around me.

Eebon stood in front of me and repeated, "Bring what we seek, Ko-ru-ku."

Suddenly I was wrenched from the mountain nest. Eebon's final, haunting, "RAWK" all I could hear through the biting wind.

Chapter Thirteen

Eebon quickly faded from view. As we flew through the frigid mountain air, tears froze on my cheek. My bracelet. What had I done? I craned my neck but couldn't see Mercy or Coyne anywhere. Then a mound of green ground reached up to grab me. Suddenly I was standing off-kilter in knee-deep grass, my ankle throbbing from the cold. Around me were soft green rolling hills, grass undulating like ocean waves in the breeze. In a moment, Mercy was beside me, then Coyne, and the giant Corvie disappeared into the clouds above us.

Coyne and I were still catching our breath, our eyes wide and faces bright red from the wild ride.

"You did it, Kyra! You did it!" Mercy's eyes lit up. She danced around and around through the field before embracing me.

"Are you kidding?" I pulled away from her. "Now we have to find what the Corvie seek *and* Mom. And since I traded my bracelet away there's absolutely no chance that the chimera can help us. Ever. Why didn't you stop me?"

"I tried!" Mercy said, pointing an accusatory claw at Coyne. "If it weren't for the human, we wouldn't have to pay the ransom for his life. "

"My life? I think Eebon was talking about you," he accused.

"Coyne's rotten heart betrayed him. He's a Thresher."

"What's that?" I asked, annoyed. Clearly, the truce was over.

"The Threshers are the humans who stole the Plains from my ancestors. They killed the Plains Raturro, stole their land, their homes. That is another reason why there is a war. Majellan's family was once Plains Raturro and only wants what was taken from them."

"All that happened a long time ago. Before I was born. Before my parents were even born," said Coyne.

"Maybe I should've let Eebon keep you both," I said under my breath.

"It is said the Corvie have lost one of their own and they search for it far and wide every day." Mercy cocked her head. "They will never rest until it's found. That's all I know."

"But the Corvie are huge. How could they lose a bird that size? Surely they could find it better than we could? Where on Earth will we look?" I asked.

"Earth?" asked Coyne.

"Never mind." Ugh. Why had I agreed to such an impossible task?

"This way." Mercy sniffed the air. "I shall ask at the Nestling if anyone has heard of the lost Corvie."

"Wait a minute. I thought the Corvie were taking us to Murch City?" I scanned the vast grassy valley and beyond. No city.

"Deep Nestling," she said, pointing to a low mountain resembling a Raturro head with two pointy ears. She twitched her own ears and smiled, obviously happy to be home.

"But—why did the Corvie drop us here?"

"We cannot go into Thane's Reach blind," Mercy said, already marching towards home. "We must make a plan first, get supplies, and get help."

She was right. We did need help, and I hoped somehow we would stumble upon the lost Corvie along the way. But Coyne only dug his boot heel into the soft grass.

"What now?"

"A Raturro nest? Really?" he said with a sigh. "She planned this."

I challenged him. "You're not afraid of a few little rats, are you?"

As we climbed the rolling hills towards the mountain with two peaks, the grass gave way to a gentle forest where the trees were full of large golden nuts and brown fuzzy fruit with juicy orange centres. We found berry brambles and long green onions with big pink flowers on top. Mercy pulled a handful of fat onions and handed them to me like a bouquet.

"We'll soon be home," she said as she munched an onion with gusto.

Coyne and I stuffed our pockets with nuts. Thankful for something to do as we walked, we peeled off their speckled shells and crunched their hard centres. Mercy ran ahead while I hung back with Coyne. After working together and laying their differences aside, I thought they were becoming friends. It reminded me of history lessons in school where people fought wars that lasted hundreds of years and even forgot what they were fighting for. Coyne may have left the war with the Raturro because he was a farmer and didn't want to fight, but what had he done that Eebon could sense in him?

"Roasted roots and berry sauce!" Mercy said, her nose twitching. "Do you smell it?"

"I can't smell a thing," I said. Coyne also shook his head.

"We're close. So close!" She scampered away over a small ridge. Trudging after her, we reached the base of the mountain but Mercy was nowhere to be found.

"Mercy?" I called. No answer.

"Too bad. Looks like we've lost her." Coyne grinned. "If we cut down that valley we'll be in Murch City in no time."

"She's got to be here somewhere." Beyond the ridge, the path grew rocky and led to a sheer cliff face. Was she hiding amidst the large boulders at the bottom of the scree? I was just about to give up when I detected an odor like sour cabbage. Past the biggest boulders, it faded, so I backtracked. It grew stronger again near a shadowy opening in the cliff face.

"Mercy?" My voice echoed into a deep cave. Placing my hands on the striped rock, I was shocked to find the database had disappeared. Along with my bracelet, I had lost the flow of information.

"Kyra! I ran up ahead with the good news. They shall all be so excited to meet you!" Mercy's head popped out of the cave and her soft warm paws grasped my hand. I waved a reluctant Coyne over and together we approached the cave entrance. As Mercy pulled me between the rocks, I reached back for Coyne's hand. It was a tight squeeze as Mercy pulled us along through the darkness.

I groped blindly along the narrow tunnel walls, and my hair snagged on the rough rock above. I stifled a giggle when I heard Coyne bump his head and grumble.

"Whoa!" I was amazed when we rounded a corner. The tunnel had grown more spacious and large aquamarine coloured crystals illuminated our way. I stopped a moment to touch their smooth surfaces, thankful for their light. Below me, the hard ground gave way to a softer substance—a mixture of fur, twigs, and rags.

"Mm, do you smell that?" said Mercy. Something delicious amidst the musk of dirty fur and burning oil. There was also a strange, high hum, like the sound of millions of insects at night.

Emerging from the tunnel into a huge, well-lit cavern, we were confronted by hundreds, maybe thousands of Raturro, big and small, young and old, all staring at us with those big brown doe eyes. Most were a pale grey like Mercy, with pinkish ears and long tails, but some had patches of white and black on their faces. I smiled and hoped they were all friendly.

Coyne stayed close by my side. "I've never seen so many rats," he whispered, incredulous.

Mercy turned excitedly to the silent, waiting rats. "She rescued me at the slave market." The crowd let out a collective gasp and as they whispered to each other, the hum returned.

"Tell them who you are." Mercy raised a paw and the Raturro fell silent.

I stepped forward and gave a nervous wave. Mercy elbowed me.

"Uh. Hi. I'm Kyra Murch." I held my breath wondering what would happen next. Then a rousing cheer went up through the crowd of Raturro. As the mass of grey fur closed in on me, Coyne grabbed me protectively. Claws touched my clothing, my hair. Coyne's too. There was much back-patting and hugging and infant rats being shoved into my arms. I peered into some adorable little rat faces.

As quickly as the wave of Raturro had crashed over me, it ebbed away. As if on cue, the mass of grey fur opened a pathway through the crowd. I looked at Mercy for direction and she nodded towards the path. I walked through the appreciative throng and the smallest rat children who were brave enough still reached for my jeans with their tiny pink paws. I giggled nervously. Coyne followed, scowling.

Ahead on a rocky outcrop sat a large white rat. The aged rat could see out over the mass of Raturro and I followed her gaze. It was then that I noticed the cavern walls. They were covered in intricate drawings and carvings—rats doing heroic deeds, portraits, and scenes of rat families. One drawing in particular surprised me and I almost ran to it.

"Chimera!" I exclaimed and all the Raturro shrieked and squeaked in fear. The chimera was drawn in dark colours, browns and reds, and the goat and lion heads had fierce fangs—a puddle of raw red pooled beneath it, like blood. I instinctively touched my wrist where my bracelet once sat. As I stood before the chimera's image, the cavern fell silent. I wondered if I'd ever see her again.

Mercy nudged me back towards the ancient rat. Standing before the white Raturro, I remembered the word 'prostrate' so I bowed down on the floor and put my forehead on the soft dirt. A peal of laughter started. I glanced up, and Mercy's eyes had grown big in wonder. Coyne just shook his head at me.

"Um, Kyra?" whispered Mercy.

"Up, child," said the ancient Raturro, waving a gnarled paw at me. "We do not ask for ceremony here in Deep Nestling. We are all equal. We are Raturro." All the Raturro started to speak at once and their voices echoed through the cavern in a cacophony, but when the white rat waved her paw, there was immediate silence.

Mercy helped me up. "Kyra, this is our Eldest Elder, Brae, who gives us wise counsel and passes the stories to our children. She will make a new story tonight and soon all Raturro will know of your brave deeds."

Mercy turned to the crowd, "Kyra swam the Soulcatcher, commanded the chimera, and befriended the Corvie."

At the mention of the Corvie, the Raturro shrieked in fear.

"This is our friend Coyne," I said, staring at Mercy. "He is also brave and helped to save Mercy." Coyne shuffled his feet behind me.

Brae held up her paw once more. "Both humans are welcome in the nest. From now until eternity they will have a home in Deep Nestling. Welcome, Kyra. Welcome, Coyne." A cheer went up from the crowd. Brae looked pleased. "What are we waiting for? It's feast time. We must declare this a day of celebration!"

A deafening roar erupted from the crowd. "But—" I was pulled by Mercy towards the white rat. Coyne grinned in disbelief at the scene.

"You must sit with the Eldest Elder and tell all you know about how you came here, where you have been. Everything." Mercy insisted. "She's the keeper of stories."

"But I have to get to Murch City. I need to find my mother and we have to find the missing Corvie," I said a bit too loudly.

Mercy froze. The Raturro fell silent and Brae regarded me with wonder.

"Mercy said you could help," I stammered.

"Murch City? It is forbidden for Deep Nestling Raturro to venture into Majellan's territory," she declared. The Raturro nodded silently.

Mercy wouldn't meet my gaze. "But I have to save the Queen!"

A soft murmur erupted from the crowd, but Brae shushed them with a look. "Mercy, what have you promised her?"

Mercy cowered a moment but as she spoke her courage returned. "She is Ko-ru-ku. I believe we should help her save the Queen. It could help to end this war."

"We must stay out of it. It could mean our demise. It is better that we—"

"Hide?" Mercy interjected. "Like mice, fearful and small?"

Brae narrowed her eyes at her. "When you are the Eldest Elder, young Mercy, then you can make decisions that affect the lives of many."

"But maybe the decisions shouldn't be left to just one. Maybe the voice of youth should be heard," Mercy continued. "Kyra rescued me, and I will return the honour."

The Raturro whispered amongst themselves for a long awkward moment, then I spoke up. "I do not want to harm any Raturro. Ever. If I ruled Antiica I would make sure the war ended and no Raturro was ever enslaved again."

The crowd erupted into cheers. Mercy's eyes sparkled. Brae could see that she was outnumbered.

"Very well," Brae declared. "Mercy, if you want to go on this impossible journey, so be it." She gazed at the crowd of Raturro. "We too shall be merchants of peace." And with that, Brae closed her eyes.

Mercy whispered to me, trying to suppress her obvious glee, "We must prepare many things for the journey, food and supplies…." Her voiced trailed off.

"What about security?" asked Coyne, who stuck to my side. "We could use some protection." It was a good concern, but Mercy never acknowledged him. She got that fierce look in her eye and I knew she didn't want him here. I really wanted them to be friends, but maybe I was asking too much. Mercy ran off into the gray mass of rats, a head taller than most of them. Her eyes almost sparkled as she disappeared into a dark tunnel.

"Kyra, come, rest after your long journey." Brae moved her ancient body off her comfortable red cushion.

"No, I couldn't." But she waved me towards the cushion covered in a mass of dirty white fur. I had no choice but to obey her. But I didn't want to be treated like royalty. It was weird. Why should some people be treated better than others?

Coyne pulled his coat off and laid it on the floor below the ledge. He sat, but remained vigilant.

I recounted our adventure for Brae. At one point, I nudged her when she appeared to be dozing, but she merely nodded and said, "Continue." The story really did sound much better in the retelling. I went on and on about Coyne's dedication and Mercy's bravery. I told her how I had felt when I first met the chimera, and Brae listened and nodded just like Mom would when I had a problem. As my story ended I let myself listen to the singing and chanting that grew around us.

A group of Raturro pups crept towards me and sat in a circle, staring at me with deep brown eyes that were far too big for their little heads. Some whimpered and moved away skittishly, but a brave few stayed, their little pink mouths hanging open. The little ones moved in closer, and I reached out and patted one of them on the head. I was suddenly embarrassed. This wasn't some pet dog I was meeting on the street. Then one of the pups scampered up my back to pat me on the head. Soon they were all patting each other on the head and squeaking in glee.

A Raturro girl approached with a tray of wooden bowls full of brightly coloured mash. She nervously placed the food in front of me and backed away as quickly as she could. Mercy, now wearing a fresh pale green dress, put her arms around the timid girl.

"Kyra, meet my fourth cousin, Lody. She's one of the greatest voices in the Nestling." Mercy nudged Lody forward, but all Lody could do was curtsy before scampering away. Mercy shooed all the little ones away from me. "Lody is Shale's niece," she whispered to me. "I have told them what Shale did, how he died."

I watched Lody walk away and felt a weight of shame wash over me, as if I was responsible for his death.

As if reading my mind Mercy said, "It's not your fault, Kyra. Shale thought he could persuade Majellan to stop his folly and paid dearly for it."

"I want to meet them. Shale's family."

"In good time. Eat, Kyra. You must have strength for our next journey."

I picked up a wooden mug and guzzled a thick cider drink. It was delicious and it lifted my spirits somewhat. Maybe Mercy was right.

I examined some sweet-smelling orange mash, but there was no fork or spoon to eat it with. I was so hungry I scooped up the warm mash with my fingers and stuck them into my mouth. The mash had a potato-like consistency with a hint of berries too. Mercy smiled at me, happy to be home.

I glanced around, suddenly remembering Coyne. He had disappeared from his post below the ledge.

"The human is getting a tour of the Nestling," Mercy said, wrinkling her nose. "He said he wanted to know where all the exits were."

"So, what's the plan?" I asked her between scoops of tasty mash.

"The rebels in Murch City have sentries all around the perimeter of the Reach and the city limits. They have even built a wall. All the humans have been driven out, so the Raturro will easily smell you long before they see you. We can't hide the fact you're human, but we can mask your terrible odor."

"*My* terrible odor?" It couldn't be any worse than the musty smelling cave.

"I may have some volunteers who will come with us."

"Really?" I asked.

"We're a peaceful tribe of Raturro—artisans, musicians, and storytellers. We have no soldiers in our midst, but there are some who want to help."

"Coyne and I can go on our own," I said, thinking of the danger.

"You will never find your way," she warned.

"I don't want any more of the Raturro hurt."

"I will never leave your side, Kyra. Besides, you know you can't trust the human."

"His name is Coyne," his voice boomed behind us. I hadn't even heard him sneak up on us. He leaned against the ledge, proud of his stealth.

"I have information that we have allies in the city," Mercy ignored him. "For years they have been planning for this day, Kyra."

"Planning? For what?" asked Coyne.

"The day Kyra saves all Raturro, of course," she exclaimed as if scolding a child. Coyne rolled his eyes, swung himself up on the ledge next to me, and grabbed a bowl of mush.

"I only came here to save my mom," I said. "Maybe this prophecy thing is wrong. How can I save *all* the Raturro?"

"We don't all know what our fate is until it happens."

Coyne scoffed at this. "Fate can get you killed."

Mercy ignored him and scampered away.

"You're really helping, Coyne," I said sarcastically.

"I know." He grinned.

Lody returned with more heaping bowls of food. Coyne accepted one, digging his fingers into it. Lody hovered a bit longer near us, but when I thanked her, she looked like she might burst into tears. The second course was even more delicious than the first. One bowl was full of sweet and creamy green mush that tasted like broccoli, if broccoli was a dessert. Coyne and I fought over a bigger bowl, full of chewy little bites of dried berry with a dark gooey centre.

"Hey, you had five already," he said.

"Mm, I can't help myself. They're awesome!"

"Oh, I can bring you more gooja treats. There are plenty of worms in the ground," squeaked Lody.

"Worms?" Coyne and I blurted at once.

Lody nodded. "Gooja berry encrusted platworm. Mm."

Careful not to insult Lody, I tried to look appreciative. I nudged Coyne. "They're, um, different. Right, Coyne?"

"Mm. Best I've ever tasted," Coyne popped another into his mouth daring me to continue.

Not to be outdone, I grabbed a handful of the delicious treats and stuffed them into my mouth. Lody's ears twitched as she wandered away, a puzzled look on her furry face. Coyne and I could easily have dissolved into fits of laughter but we kept it in; we were guests in the Nestling and we would be respectful.

The Eldest Elder was nowhere around. I felt kind of bad I had taken her seat but it did turn out to be very comfortable. Ready to explore on my own, I left Coyne to finish the food. Maze-like tunnels and caves led off the main cavern. All around me there were small groups of Raturro. Some were pups, some were elders who stopped talking as I walked by. I smiled at them all and they broke into whispers.

I found myself drawn to the wall where the image of the chimera stood. I examined the intricate drawing, which was not exactly like the real thing. My chimera was fierce, but this picture was of an evil demon. Its fangs and claws were longer, and there was a look of hatred in all the red eyes. The colours were all wrong, too. The real chimera was awash in colour and light. This chimera was dull, dark, and bloody. Seeking comfort, I put my hand on the cold stone and concentrated hard, trying to contact it.

"They say you're a Stone Traveller," said a small voice. "Is it true?" A boy about the same age as Lody stared in fear at the chimera.

"Stone Traveller?" I nodded. "But the chimera is more than that. She's a…friend." That strange pull she had over me had faded since I'd lost the bracelet. But I still yearned for the warmth I felt when she was with me.

"My grandfather drew this." He shuddered.

"Really? It's very good," I replied. The boy reached out to touch the chimera probably for the first time ever.

"It won't harm you," I said.

Still, he quickly pulled his paw away from the wall. "I'm Scat."

"I'm Kyra."

"I know. Mercy said I should take you to see Shale's family."

"Oh" was all I could say. We examined the chimera for a little longer.

"Wait a minute. Is your grandfather here?"

The boy shook his head, no.

"I just wondered if he actually saw the chimera."

"Yes, he did." Scat's face lit up. "He saw it. That's how he came to draw it. Do you want to meet my father? He has a story about it."

"Um, yes. But first I'd like to meet Shale's family." I felt my heart sink. I hoped Shale's family wouldn't want all the details of his death. I couldn't bear to cause them any more pain.

We headed up a winding tunnel and soon came to a small entrance that I had to crawl through. Scat didn't follow me. Inside was a roomful of Raturro of all sizes and ages. Each held a little clay pot with burning oil in it. The light cast an eerie gloom over the room. I sat in the soft dirt and waited, but no one spoke.

"I'm Kyra Murch," I said.

They only stared back at me.

A series of carved shelves sat in the corner of the cave. One held a rag-eared Raturro doll and a series of colourful rocks and sticks. All around it were more oil candles. It was an altar.

A wizened Raturro with kind eyes reached out her paw and rested it on my shoulder. I turned to her, unsure where to begin. On the other side of me, a middle-aged Raturro reached her paw out and touched my other shoulder.

"I'm sorry," I murmured. "I'm sorry that Shale died. I wasn't able to stop it. He spoke of his children, how he loved them so much."

"Shale is a hero to us all," said the wizened Raturro. "He was my son. Brave. Foolish. Kind."

I nodded in agreement. Then the other Raturro spoke.

"My husband left to help put an end to the war. He knew he might not return. This—" she gestured to the roomful of Raturro big and small— "is his legacy. We will tell his story for years to come."

"But Shale—" They peered at me with expectation. Was I to tell them the truth about Shale? About the torture? About my father?

As if reading my mind, the wizened Raturro squeezed my hand. "Pup," she said, "we know Shale is a hero. That is the end of his story."

I was grateful, but I also felt guilty. Lody entered the cave with two lit oil pots and silently handed one to me. All the Raturro then turned to the altar. The little Raturro doll had shiny brass buttons on its coat, just like Shale's. I would never forget Shale. I would never forget his family.

Chapter Fourteen

Scat was waiting for me outside Shale's home. I followed him but he was too quick and lost me in one of the tunnels. When I stopped and waited, sure enough, he came running back. He grabbed my hand to drag me through the underground maze.

"Father!" Scat cried. "Kyra wants to meet you! She was admiring Old Weeta's drawing of the demon." The Raturro family froze when I stooped down to enter a room no bigger than my kitchen back home. The older Raturro sat on high cushions and the little ones rolled around playing a game on the soft floor.

I crouched down in the middle of the room as a portly Raturro with a tuft of white hair between his ears lumbered forward and extended his paw for me to shake. "This is how it's done in Murch, no?" Then, I had to shake everyone's paws. One of the young pups climbed up my back and patted me on the head. News traveled fast in the Nestling.

"Please, it's our freshest mull," said Scat's mother, Pribble. I accepted the steaming mug and inhaled the sweet scent.

Weeta the Younger, Scat's father, sat beside me and was excited to share his story. "My father, Old Weeta, was a young servant in Thane's Reach. He was very proud of his job, where he would set the table for the Thane and his guests and clean up when the meal was finished. He told me of the great love of food the humans had and how they wasted as much as they ate. So there were always fat Raturro in the Reach as we never let anything go to waste." He patted his round stomach, giggling. His laugh was contagious.

"When Father finished cleaning at night, he would sometimes observe the monster asleep on the wall of the great dining hall. The monster slept a lot in those days, all through dinner and after the Thane went to bed. So Old Weeta would study it, memorize every curve and feature. Until one night, as he sat in front of it, mesmerized, the great beast opened its red, glowing eyes." All the pups shrieked.

"Then what happened?" I asked.

"Well, my father fainted dead away."

"Oh, she is frightening when you first meet her," I said apologetically.

"But when he woke up, he found the most incredible thing. The Thane stood in front of the chimera, his bracelets shining in its light and the chimera was sucked into the Thane. It disappeared off the wall and seemed to float right inside of him. Your grandfather turned to my father and said, 'There, it won't frighten you again'."

"My grandfather?" I said, bewildered both by the story and the discovery of yet another relative.

"Yes, Thane Ettwan, but he died long before you were born, when your father was still a young man."

"Wait, so he wore two bracelets?"

Weeta the Younger twitched his nose, thinking. "Yes, the story has always said two bracelets. They are the source of the Thane's power. Do you have them?"

"My mother gave me one for protection, but I gave it to the Corvie in exchange for our freedom." I glanced at my bare wrist. "My father has the other one." But he warned me never to wear two. Why?

"Hm. I shall consult the Elders and see if there are any more stories of the bracelets, Ko-ru-ku. If this is what you wish?"

"Oh, yes. Please. Anything you know about the chimera would be most welcome."

"You mean you know nothing about it?" Pribble shot Weeta an uncomfortable glance.

"No, why?"

"Has no one told you of the Stone Wars?" said Weeta.

"Stone Wars?"

The room went silent. Even the little ones stopped moving and stared at me. I felt my throat go thick.

"Come, pups, let your father talk," said Pribble, as she shooed them away.

"It was many generations ago, of your grandfather's line. The old Thanes used their power, er, unwisely," Weeta began. "They drove us away from our homes, out of the surrounding countryside and barely a pup was spared. Raturrocide."

I reeled.

"But worst of all was the red-eyed demon. The Thane unleashed it at will, murdering thousands of Raturro with no care for families or children."

"Red-eyed demon," I whispered. No!

"The Thane's army carried a magical stone and the chimera came through it. The chimera was hated and feared by all." He paused. "It still is to this day."

"Are you sure? It couldn't have been the chimera that I—could it?"

He nodded yes. "It was a tool of war. It still is. Your father was a fair Thane at first, and the Raturro forgave but never forgot the Stone Wars. The problem with hatred is that it is passed along from generation to generation. Just when you think the peace will last…."

I bowed my head, feeling the weight of my family's shame. Thanking Weeta, I made my way back down a dark tunnel. My brain ached, and I stumbled into the darkest corridors, avoiding the Raturro. Mom had never even mentioned my grandfather before, or the wars.

Ahead was a bluish glow and I felt drawn to its light. Soon I was in an immense cavern full of crystals reflecting blue light all around me. Climbing over the sharp stones, I found a flat crystal in the centre where the light was brightest, an oasis amidst the hustle and bustle in the Nestling. I folded down on it, closed my eyes, and breathed deeply.

"Kyraa!"

"Chimera?" I looked up half expecting to see her, but it was only Mercy.

"Kyra. You mustn't be in here. This is for the Eldest Elder only. No human must set foot in here."

"It's so beautiful. Peaceful. What is it?"

"The Cave of Light. It brings wise thoughts to our Elders. And when they have passed on, they are laid to rest on that very rock you sit on."

"You mean the dead? Oh, I'm sorry. I didn't mean—I didn't know," I said, jumping up off the rock. I felt my face flush with embarrassment.

"Come," she said.

But I wasn't ready to leave. "Weeta told me what the chimera did. The Stone Wars. I'm so sorry. I had no idea."

"You needn't apologize for the past," Mercy reached for my hand. "You are the one who will save us all, Ko-ru-ku. You are the one who will give us a future."

"No, you're wrong about me." Tears welled up in my eyes. "I trusted the chimera, but it's a killing machine. Why didn't you say something? How can you even be my friend?"

Mercy twisted her apron with her claws. "It is only as good as the person who controls it. The chimera is also imprisoned."

"What? It is? I don't understand this place. Why did my father even bring me here?" I was so confused. Tears burned my cheeks, and I felt like I could explode. "I can't let you take me to Murch City. I can't put any more Raturro in danger. This was a stupid idea. All of it."

Mercy gave me a look of pity. "Oh, Kyra, there is so much wrong on Antiica that you can do no further damage. You can only help it get better."

She pulled a rag out of her pocket and dabbed my face.

"The chimera isn't just a weapon. It's a tool. If anyone can put it to good use, then you can."

"You sound like Brae."

Mercy grinned. "That is the highest compliment anyone has ever paid me."

As we returned to the great cavern I was surprised to see all the Raturro sitting in a big circle around a platform. Excitement and the tasty aroma of food were in the air.

"Why didn't you tell me about the Stone Wars?" I whispered to Coyne when I joined him on the floor.

"How could you not know?" he hissed. "Every kid is told about the Stone Wars by their parents or they learn it in school."

Why had my parents kept so many secrets from me?

Before Brae arrived, a group of young rats ran out onto the platform to perform a death-defying circus act. They were flipping and climbing on top of each other's shoulders, doing amazing feats of balance and skill. There was comedy too when two smaller almost identical Raturro ran out to try and copy the bigger ones.

A horn sounded and the acrobats rolled away. Two hooded figures appeared from an adjacent cave. On long poles, they dangled a shadow puppet resembling a Raturro. As it got closer, I could see it was an actual Raturro skin. Its head was still intact, its eyes glass orbs. The pink tail had grown dull while the claws had been sharpened. Another two hooded figures joined them carrying a second skin. The figures danced around the circle as the crowd chanted and growled in reverence. I couldn't keep my eyes off those skins. Had they really been living breathing Raturro? I watched the crowd's fascination as the skins appeared to writhe and dance.

Then I had a thought. I nudged Coyne. "That's what we need to get us into Thane's Reach. A disguise."

"That's never going to happen," he said, disgusted.

Lody took the stage. No longer looking the fragile, fearful girl of earlier, her intense brown eyes lit up as she began to sing the Raturro anthem:

Deep in the Nestling, there's a home that I love.
There's a mother and father and twenty young pups.
It's said it's the bestest of all the rats' homes,
For we're never a-wantin' and we never look up.
Deep in the Nestling, there's a home that I love....

All the Raturro joined in on the chorus, not one singer out of tune. The voices rose in harmony and the cavern amplified the sweet sound. I was transported to Earth, to my bedroom. Mom often sang me to sleep when I was little. She would wrap her warm arms around me and cocoon me in love and safety. I suddenly missed Earth very much.

Lody finished her song and while the cavern was quiet, there were a few sobs from the crowd. A couple of fearless baby rats crawled over, some to sit in my lap, others in Coyne's lap. Even he couldn't push them away.

Brae limped into the circle. Her cushion was pulled out onto the platform and she took centre stage. The crowd hushed.

"As long as there has been suffering amongst the Raturro of every clan, there has been a tale, a legend, a prophecy. It started many seasons ago, not long after the Raturro lost their land, lost their children. Perhaps it was the dream of a small child that started it, or perhaps it was an Elder's last breath, but wherever it started it rippled through the Raturro like a song of freedom. Aye."

"Aye!" the crowd responded.

"This song of freedom was not a lie," she continued, "not a hope, or an untruth, it was a dream. And now this prophecy has come true. Though she has done heroic deeds already, Kyra, the Last Murch, has come to Deep Nestling and here her story begins anew."

A deafening cheer went up amongst the Raturro.

"She is the last of her line of Stone Travellers, the smallest, the youngest, the weakest, but she is the most courageous Murch of all. I believe she has the heart of a Raturro."

I drew in a sharp breath. I did feel closer to the Raturro than my father or his cause. Yes, I was weak. I was small. But I wasn't going to let that stop me.

Another cheer from the crowd. The rat pups had fallen asleep in my lap. I couldn't move or I'd wake them.

Brae wove her story into a tale I barely recognized, casting me as some sort of champion: I was fierce and humble, brave and kind. It was embarrassing but I suddenly didn't feel so small. Mercy sniffled next to me and so did all of the Raturro. When it came to the part where we were high on the mountain with the Corvie, I, too, began to choke back my tears remembering the promise I'd made.

"We've got to leave at once for Murch City," I jumped up, startling the sleeping pups. "I haven't finished what I came here to do."

"Ko-ru-ku," called Brae.

"Ko-ru-ku," chanted the crowd. Mercy was on her feet beside me, pulling me towards Brae.

"No, Mercy, we have to go. I have to find Mom and the missing Corvie or I'll never get my bracelet back."

"Ko-ru-ku! Ko-ru-ku!"

Mercy continued chanting with the others. I glanced over at Coyne and was amazed to see he held two sleeping pups in his arms. We shared a look. If he could find something to love about the Raturro, there was hope.

"I have to stop this war!" I couldn't tell if anyone heard me, but I knew I would no longer sit back and see the Raturro suffer. I wouldn't let them down. Not after what my family had done. I was beginning to understand Majellan's anger towards my family. Maybe I was on the wrong side.

CHAPTER FIFTEEN

"Mercy, where's Coyne?" I asked as I applied a hideous, bitter-smelling liquid to my skin in order to disguise my human scent. Maybe he'd changed his mind about accompanying us to Murch City and slipped away during the night. I shivered. It was a cold morning, but I was also worried he was gone. I understood that he needed to get home, but I didn't want to finish my journey without him. Mercy only shrugged.

I gazed around at the assembled rats. I had hoped for the biggest and strongest of the Raturro for our journey, but our group now consisted of Lody, Scat, and the two young acrobat twins who performed last night. Peep and Gnarls were play fighting and rolling along the dirt floor of the cavern and I had no idea how useful they would be.

"The Rat-gah are heroes to the Nestling," said Brae, supervising the donning of the ceremonial rat skin. As the hollowed-out head was fit over mine, I barely felt human anymore.

"Elder Brae, I don't mean any offence, but perhaps I was wrong about this."

"Kyra, it is the will of the Rat-gah. You must take them to battle with you. The ancestors will be proud that they helped free all Raturro."

"It's a great honour to wear the ceremonial Rat-gah," Mercy reassured me, as she lovingly stroked the fur that now enveloped me. "Ah, Rat-gah. This was our wisest Elder. And wearing it will make you wise, Ko-ru-ku." She added a shawl to help conceal my face.

As we turned to leave, Weeta ran up to us, panting. "Kyra, I've asked all the Elders what they remembered about my father's story and they all say the same. Two bracelets. Maybe you can find out more from the Murch City Raturro. You can mention my father's name. I'm sure the city rats would recognize it," he added proudly.

Nodding at Weeta in thanks, I wished I'd asked Dad more about the bracelets.

"We must go now," Mercy interrupted.

I followed, dragging my new tail behind me.

We trekked along a dark tunnel, a shortcut to the city. Already I missed the sun and fresh air, but soon the path sloped upwards and there was a bright light up ahead. The outline of a large Raturro stood in the cave entrance and I clenched my jaw, suddenly afraid it was Majellan.

Coyne was also dressed in a Rat-gah. My heart jumped. He was still here! When we saw each other up close, we couldn't help but laugh at how we looked.

"Kyra!" Mercy scowled. "You must not disrespect the Rat-gah!" Frightened by her tone, the twins crawled on all fours to hide behind Lody and Scat. "Those who wear it are honoured. They are respected."

I tilted my head up and pulled the scarf down so I could meet her gaze. "I'm sorry, Mercy. It was nervous laughter. Honest." Mercy harrumphed and we followed her outside.

The sun was bright and the day beautiful as we left Deep Nestling. I was dressed as a giant rat and I was ready. Even Coyne seemed lighter. Behind us, Lody and Scat held paws and giggled over some secret they shared.

For hours we travelled down the side of the mountain and soon we could see Murch City in the distance. There was a huge shimmering structure on a hill in the middle of the great valley where the city sprawled out, its streets like tentacles reaching out for prey.

"That's Thane's Reach," said Mercy. Even before she said it, I felt the hair stand up on my neck. The castle gleamed in the sun. Regal, like a storybook castle. But there was also something foreboding about it. I thought of Mom, trapped someplace inside and shuddered. I hoped Majellan had not hurt her.

"Let's get going," I said, suddenly worried, as Peep and Gnarls cartwheeled right into me, knocking me down.

"You stupid rats! I'm trying to save my mom and you're just playing around! Why are you even here?"

The twins scurried behind Mercy's skirts.

Ashamed at my outburst, I stormed past them down the hill, my eyes never leaving the city sprawled below us.

"We'll find her, Kyra. I promise," said Coyne, quickly at my side. I peered up at him through the Rat-gah, relieved he was seeing this through. He gave me an awkward pat on the back and we continued on down the hill dragging our tails behind us.

Beyond the city, the land became rolling farmland. I'd come in one big circle and was still no further ahead. Over there was where I first met Coyne in the little Raturro cottage. I glanced skyward, wondering how we would find the missing Corvie anywhere near here.

"We'll dip down into the next valley and stay the night," said Mercy, slipping in beside me. "Best to arrive in Murch when the markets are open in the morning. There's less chance of unwanted attention. We will be stopped and questioned at some point by the Raturro Guard and we will say that we are travelling minstrels. We have come to Murch to entertain Majellan."

"And what about your friends down there? Will they be able to get us into the Reach?"

"We won't know until we get into the city," she answered, looking thoughtful. "There have been all sorts of rumours about what the rebels have done to the Reach. It's been many years since I've been inside."

"Coyne, have you been there before?"

"When I was a little boy." Coyne nodded. "I don't really remember much. But I do know that you can see Thane's Reach from almost every street in the city."

I reached down and grabbed my heavy tail. Even if my disguise fooled them, I could hardly demand to see Mom.

Seeing the Reach didn't spark any memories whatsoever. An entire kingdom lay ahead of me and none of it seemed familiar. Was that really where I was born? I would have been about four years old when we left. Old enough to remember a childhood, but where was it?

I led Mercy and the rest down the hill, forging ahead. Behind me, Lody started singing a ballad and the rest of them joined in. It took a few verses before I realized the song was about me.

The Last Murch came to Nestling, so deep in the dirt.

She saved our dear Mercy and never got hurt.
We've waited a lifetime and now that she's here,
We're singing this ratsong to tell her she's dear.

Lody continued singing to entertain us as we travelled through most of the day and her singing lifted my spirits. The young ones danced and pranced and even Coyne hummed a tune now and then.

"I've found a place for us to spend the night," Mercy said, returning from scouting ahead. "It's deserted, and we'll be safe there."

"What sort of place?" I asked.

"You'll see," she said cryptically.

Soon we came to an overgrown orchard. Vines with dark purple blooms crept up over yellow barked trees, strangling their trunks. "We're here!" Mercy declared. "Let's camp for the night."

"I'll go ahead and check if it's safe," Coyne offered.

"No need. I've already done it," she said, pointing him towards a small, shimmery lake. "Peep and Gnarls can find fish for our dinner." With Scat following, the twins ran straight for the water but only started splashing about. Would we go hungry?

"I'll stay here and help," Coyne laughed, shaking his head.

Lody hummed to herself as she wandered off to gather herbs and fruits nearby.

"Come," said Mercy, a glimmer in her eye. A worn stone path led us through a garden full of fragrant trees and gnarled shrubs. After pushing back branches and stepping over fallen trees, the thick shrubbery finally opened up to a clearing.

And then I saw it. The tree in my photo. The monkey puzzle tree! It stood tall above the others and dwarfed a stone cottage behind it. Goosebumps raised on my arms.

"I've been here before, haven't I?"

"Oh, yes, Kyra. This is your summer home. This is the Cress." Mercy grinned.

"The Cress?" Yes, there was something familiar about that name. I ran past Mercy and stopped at an old wooden gate lying at an angle, its hinges rusted away. I remembered holding onto it and swinging myself back and forth. The front yard was abloom with flowers of all shapes, colours, and sizes—blazing red showy blooms and delicate pink things with funny little faces. I remembered them too.

I glanced back at Mercy. She waved me ahead to discover the quaint stone cottage for myself. When I opened the arched door, I could smell dust and wooden beams, stone and the fireplace, but most of all, my childhood. It was real!

I pushed back the Rat-gah head and pulled away the shawl. Glancing around the living room, there was a dusty old couch and broken down table. Faded wallpaper showed where pictures had once hung. I crept up the staircase, knowing what I would find at the top.

First door on the left.

I pushed the door open into my old bedroom. A single iron bed sat in the corner, its blankets long gone. A chest of heavy wood and child-sized table and chairs sat near a fireplace. Kneeling down, I wiped dust off the tabletop to discover a faded alphabet. This was where Mercy and I had played. Our favorite spot for tea parties, dolls, and painting. We had laughed and sung together. It all came back to me and a surge of happiness went through me. It was once mine.

I ran out into the hallway to open the next door, where I knew I'd find my parents' room and their big four-poster double bed. I half-expected to see them, remembering the mornings when I jumped on their soft bed and crawled in under downy covers. Now, the bed frame was in pieces, and the dusty mattress sagged against the mildewed wall.

Slowly, I walked back downstairs. I could almost smell the toast browning in front of the fire. We'd sit outside in the sun and laugh. Mercy and I would run through the long grass and pull flowers out of the garden and wear them like crowns—all under the watchful eye of my parents. Once Mom and Dad and I had all been together and happy. Now I was sure.

I went back outside into the sun and stared at the monkey puzzle tree for a long, long time. Its elongated, dark green branches held spiky triangular-shaped leaves. The branches hung down like monkey arms and curled up at the bottom. The outstretched hands beckoned me—come play! I stood alone with my memories. My house. My monkey puzzle tree. At the base, I found a flat stone covered with dirt and leaves. I scraped off the debris, exposing a smooth octagonal stone. Excited, I pulled the photo out of my pocket. This is where we would have stood for the photo.

The Cress Stone. The name popped into my head. It was important. The Cress Stone had been my favorite place to sit in the sun and pretend. Once upon a time, I was a little monkey who lived under the big monkey tree king. I would scamper about and obey the king's orders like a good little monkey would. I would guard the monkey home, the monkey yard, the monkey tree, and keep the Cress Stone safe.

I had an image of my father bending down and resting his hand on the stone. I stood next to him as he told me something important. "Promise me you will keep it safe," he said. My little hand touched the stone, and then he placed his hand over mine.

I placed my hand on the flat stone now but had no idea what it was made of. The database remained closed. I glanced up at the tree again, at the cottage, and vowed that someday I'd come back and fix everything. I'd make the Cress a home again. I would live there with Mom and Dad. We'd clean up the garden, get new furniture for the house, and never, ever have Raturro slaves.

I swallowed back the lump in my throat, pulled out of my reverie by Lody's sweet singing and the laughter of Mercy, Scat, Peep, and Gnarls getting closer to the cottage. I quickly covered the Cress Stone with leaves as they strolled through the gate, soaking wet, a pile of fish in their paws. Lody had an apron full of greens and Coyne had filled his coat with fruit and nuts. We would feast tonight.

With Mercy's help, Coyne and I removed our heavy Rat-gah. She carefully laid them in a corner of the living room and stroked the fur all the while whispering reassurances. It was a relief to feel human again.

Soon Lody had the fireplace ablaze and Mercy found a large skillet to fry up the fish. As the fish simmered, she told us about how her mother, Pippamin, had done the same thing, in the very same house when she had worked for Mom and Dad. Her mother always talked about how it was a holiday for them too. Even after they returned to Deep Nestling and no longer worked for the Thane, Mercy's mom thought of it fondly.

When she was old enough, Mercy had left to work for a human family but then the war started and she was enslaved. She wasn't allowed to return home or to Murch City. It was then that Pippamin died. Mercy couldn't say more, but her eyes clouded over. I was sorry I didn't remember Pippamin, but it was heartening to know that there was a time when my parents sat to dinner with friendly Raturro.

"And we'd all sit at the table as equals. Humans and rats." Mercy looked to Coyne and held a cracked dinner plate out to him, as if apologizing for the way she had treated him. Coyne nodded in thanks. I grinned at Mercy, and I knew she was my best friend. Always.

Full, we all lay around on the floor in front of the fireplace. It had cooled down with evening and it felt good to be with friends. One by one they curled up into balls and fell asleep. Soon only Coyne and I were left awake. I stared into the fire and let the memory of the cottage seep into me. I felt four years old again. I imagined sitting on Mom's knee as she combed my hair. I could see Dad stoking the fire, and then sitting next to us, his arm around Mom. I didn't know if it was a real memory, but I sure wanted it to be.

"You okay?" Coyne asked. He moved closer to me and we bumped shoulders. "Are you sure you're ready for tomorrow?"

"I dunno. I don't even want to think of what might happen when we get there."

"Yeah, I know what you mean." He sighed heavily. "This must've been a nice place to live."

"Yeah, it's special. I wish…" I trailed off. "I dunno. I want my family to be happy again. To be together."

Our hands rested on the floor between us, pinky fingers almost touching.

"But?"

"But knowing what I know about my father, about the war, I don't see how it could ever be the same."

Coyne's pinky finger looped over mine and we both held on tight.

Chapter Sixteen

We are watching; we are near.

"Huh?" I jumped up off the floor and looked around for the source of the voice.

"Chimera? Are you there? Chimera?" I rubbed my hands over the great stone fireplace, but it was cold. I felt nothing. *Chimera?*

Coyne stirred on the floor. "Kyra? What's wrong?"

Mercy's ears pricked up even though her eyes were still closed.

"The chimera—I heard her. She was here. She's trying to reach me," I said.

Coyne was surprised. "Did you see it?"

"No. Maybe it was just a dream." My shoulders slumped.

Mercy and the others woke up.

"Mercy, you know more about the chimera than anyone. Is there any other way I can contact it?"

"Without the bracelet? No. All I know is that you must sit a long time with your thoughts. You must learn what's inside of yourself before you can call it properly."

I looked at her, confused. "I don't know what that means."

"You need to know who you are."

"But I don't know who I am. I came here and suddenly Dad is this Thane and there are pictures of me I hardly remember and giant birds and talking rats. No offence. I just want to go back to the way things were," I said. "I just want to find Mom."

"We must get to the city," she said.

Coyne picked up the Rat-gah, got down on one knee, and held it out me. I reached out and stroked the offering like I'd seen Mercy do.

"Let's do this thing," he said.

I picked up the Rat-gah and pulled it over my head.

After an hour trekking along a well-worn path through the forest, sweat trickled down my neck and back. I dragged behind our troupe. The heavy fur of the Rat-gah might've been great in a snowstorm on Earth, but not in the intense Antiica sun. Coyne never complained.

In unison, the Raturro froze in their tracks, their ears on high alert. "What is it?" asked Coyne.

"Shhhh!" whispered Mercy, her nose twitching. "Humans! A patrol!"

"This close to Murch?" asked Coyne.

I couldn't see or hear much in my disguise, but I trusted her senses. There was no way Dad's army would stop me from entering the Reach.

"Hide!" I said. I dove for a clearing in the trees and rolled down into a ditch. The others followed except Gnarls who snuck ahead to spy on the patrol. Who knew what the army would do if they found us? As we blended into the shadows, I heard a whimper from Lody; she was terrified. I reached over and took her trembling paw in my hand. Within moments, Gnarls crept back and whispered something to Mercy, then he blended in with the rest of us.

Above us on the path thundered the familiar footfalls of army boots. My heart thundered in my chest. We nearly walked right into them. We lay still long after the sound of boots faded away.

"I bet they're looking for you, Kyra," Mercy whispered. "What do you want to do?"

"We're too close to turn back now," I said. I slipped the Rat-gah off my face, gasping for air. The fear of getting caught had made me hold my breath. "We keep going."

"Yep," Coyne agreed and pushed my Rat-gah back down.

We avoided the path and kept to the thick forest. My Raturro friends were on high alert, noses and ears to the wind. The danger of our mission had hit home, along with the very real possibility of another patrol up ahead—human or Raturro.

After a few more hours of sneaking through the forest, we spied houses and farms. Soon the forest ended and we couldn't avoid the dusty streets on the outskirts of Murch.

As we got closer to the city, we came upon the rebel roadblock set up to keep out the human army. Before us was an imposing stone wall where thousands of Raturro swiftly worked to build it higher and thicker. Armed rebel guards paced the wall, searching for any sign of a human invasion. I couldn't blast my way through like Dad might with his tanks, but I hoped a sneaky, unseen attack would do.

As our group approached the entryway, we were stopped and inspected. A portly Raturro guard lumbered around our group, sniffing us. As the guard got closer to Coyne and me,

Gnarls and Peep did cartwheels and leapfrogged over each other. The guards laughed, distracted. As we inched forward through the gate, I hoped they wouldn't notice I was human.

Once safely inside the city gates, I felt my shoulders relax and I nudged Coyne. Mercy's foul-smelling oil had done the trick: we were Raturro.

Coyne was right. No matter what street we were on, I could see Thane's Reach towering above us, shimmering in the sun. The castle was made of white limestone and polished black slate on the roof. There were soaring towers and parapets, round windows, and shuttered doors leading out onto elegant balconies. It finally hit me that the fairytale castle had also been my home. I had no idea what it looked like before, but now a series of bright red flags hung around the castle—all emblazoned with a fierce Raturro head in profile. I tamped back the emotion I felt, determined to stay strong for what was ahead.

Through the folds in my shawl I glimpsed tall, dark grey City Raturro and paler short Raturro from other parts of Antiica mingling in the cobbled streets. A fat Raturro mother scurried past us with about a dozen pups in tow. One stopped near me and squeaked a protest. "Mama, what stinks?"

Mercy put her paw on my arm to pull me along. We ducked down an alley between some brick buildings and hid behind a small shed.

"Kyra, I can smell you again," she said, worried.

"I'm sweating. The oil must be losing its strength," I said, sniffing myself.

Mercy slipped me the vial of bitter smelling oil so I could apply some more. I was getting used to the pungent, skunky aroma.

"The marketplace is up ahead. We shall soon be there." Mercy scurried away to the edge of the alley to watch for trouble.

Coyne leaned on the wall next to me and I was thankful for his company. Lody and Scat held hands, and I was kind of jealous that they had some sort of secret language.

"Coyne," I whispered. I couldn't look him in the eye because of the Rat-gah, but I knew I had to say something. He had come all this way to help me, risking his life, and delaying his return to his family on Plains.

"Hm?" he answered.

"Um, I just wanted to say thanks for all of your help."

"I haven't really done anything yet."

"Sure you have. I'm glad you came along. Without you…" I faltered.

"This is it," said Coyne. "There's no turning back now."

"Just think, we're the only humans walking the streets of Murch," I said. "Listen, I was thinking…what if I just took this thing off and marched through the streets? I could ask to see Majellan and tell him we want peace."

"What? I thought we were here for your mom," he said.

"This whole mess is because of my family."

Mercy had snuck up beside us and heard our conversation. "Kyra, you mustn't take off the Rat-gah. The City Raturro are different from Deep Nestling. Remember: they are at war."

She was right. It was a crazy idea.

"You no longer have the stench of a human," said Mercy, her nose atwitch. Coyne groaned from inside his Rat-gah.

"What's wrong?" she asked.

"Nothing. Ready?" I asked.

Mercy nodded. Gnarls and Peep stood at attention and saluted. Scat and Lody, paws still intertwined, moved in closer and squeaked a response.

We were as ready as we'd ever be. Coyne and I stooped our bodies to blend in, looking as Raturro-like as possible. Scat and Lody took the lead, and Mercy's paw held my arm in a tight grasp as we shuffled towards the bustling market.

I could only see the ground. A blur of Raturro hind paws skittered past us. The crowd grew thick, and the odor of cooking and food told me that we had arrived at the market. Mercy didn't want to arouse suspicion by asking around for her cousin Yurl, so we would make him come to us. We were going to put on a show.

At one end of the busy marketplace stood an elevated stage. Some Raturro had set up shop on the edges of it, selling nuts and onions. Once we climbed up on the stage they took their wares and moved away. I took a deep breath, hoping our plan would work.

Mercy nodded to us all and we took our positions. She faced the small group of rats that watched us with interest. "Raturro families, we come to make your day a pleasant one. We are Deep Nestling Raturro." Squeaks and murmurs came from the audience, and more shoppers stopped what they were doing and turned to watch.

Gnarls and Peep started their routine. Peep climbed up on Gnarls' shoulders and they pretended to lose their balance. Teetering and reeling, Peep nearly fell off each time, recovering at the last second. Then Scat scampered up their bodies to the top of their tower. The audience "oohed" when Lody crawled up to stand on Scat's shoulders. Coyne and I stood near the back, pretending to be aged Raturro, too old to perform. Then Lody started to sing. It was another Raturro folk song, but with a faster beat that soon had the audience stamping their feet. Somewhere nearby a flute joined in, then a fiddle. Soon, the entire market was dancing and stomping.

Suddenly a couple of Raturro jumped up on stage and danced, hooking arms with Mercy. Coyne and I were thrown into the lively folk dance, and I suddenly teetered off the edge of the stage. My Rat-gah shifted awkwardly. Then I was flung back into the dizzying dance. I grabbed Coyne and managed to pull us away from the circle of dancers.

As we caught our breath, I heard Mercy speaking to the Raturro she was dancing with. He was small, wiry, and swung her around with ease.

"Yurl, is it you?" asked Mercy.

A raspy Raturro voice answered, "Cousin, you're a long way from home."

"Yurl, it's really you!" Mercy squeaked gleefully, hugging him. "I have a valuable package to deliver. We need to get inside the Reach." She pulled him back towards Coyne and me.

"That's a tall order, cousin," he replied. "Your package must be very important."

"Ko-ru-ku," was all she said. Yurl stopped, slack-jawed. "Are you mad?"

"You must help us, Yurl," she begged. "The Last Murch will save us all."

"That is an old rats' tale. No one in the city believes—"

Mercy pulled Yurl closer until he picked up my scent. "The Rebels are everywhere," he whispered. "You should never have come into the city. You must leave at once." Then he grabbed Mercy's paws. "Listen to me, cousin. No good can come of helping humans." He turned tail and ran off into the crowd.

Coyne and I groaned, our best chance of getting into the Reach now gone. "Let's get out of here," he urged.

Mercy turned to the still teetering tower of rats and clapped her paws. Lody stopped singing and gave a little bow. The audience clapped and tittered happily.

But before we could move away, Lody called to us from the top of the tower. "Guards!"

"Quick," I said. Mercy grabbed Coyne and me, and we jumped down off the stage.

"Go left," shouted Lody as she and the others leapt off the stage and made a beeline for the guards who could be seen above the crowd. We were surrounded.

Mercy wove in and out of the market stalls. Her pace increased, then she faltered. "Oh, dear," whispered Mercy.

"What is it?" I said.

"Shhhh."

A bead of sweat ran down my nose. We took a quick turn to the left and dashed between more tables, where clay bowls and pots and mugs balanced in huge piles.

"This way. Hurry!" She pulled us in another direction until we were practically running. All around us, there were gasps and I could see Raturro hind paws scurry away from us. If Mercy and the others were caught helping humans, they would be labeled as traitors to the Raturro. I couldn't let that happen.

Suddenly, Mercy stopped and her claws dug into my arm.

"Where are you going?" A deep voice bellowed ahead of us.

"We're in the market for goods, sir," answered Mercy.

"All of you?" The voice bellowed again.

The market went quiet.

The large clawed hind paws of the rebel Raturro closed in. We had walked into a trap. I had underestimated Majellan. Somehow he was expecting us.

"Coyne," I whispered. He bumped my rat paw with his.

"On my move," Coyne whispered back.

"What Nestling are you from?" said the voice again.

Mercy didn't respond.

"Serpents!" shouted Coyne.

We had practiced this. On our trek to the city, I had insisted on a Plan B if things went sideways. And they had.

"Serpents! Serpents!" Lody and Scat roared and spooked the crowd. The market erupted into chaos.

Coyne and I followed Mercy away from the ruckus, but I tripped over something and went flying into a table of earthenware. CRASH. Everything fell to the ground including me. Coyne helped me up but the head of my Ratgah twisted upward revealing my face.

"Human!" a Raturro called out.

"The Last Murch is here!" said another. How did they know who I was?

Pups cried. Raturro squealed. And I ran into Mercy's back knocking her over.

It was the worst rescue plan ever. The Raturro Guard was almost upon us.

Coyne grabbed some large pots and hurled them in their way.

"Go," shouted Mercy, who pushed Coyne and took over throwing baskets and plates and whatever she could get her paws on. "Get her to safety."

"What about you?" I asked as Coyne grabbed my hand.

"Run," Coyne urged. We ran with all our might down a winding street, through a maze of homes and crowded stands of shoppers all gawking to see what was going on.

Soon the din of the market faded behind us. Coyne and I rounded a corner and stopped. We were both panting heavily and could barely breathe in our Rat-gah.

"We have to go back for them," I said.

"No. It's not safe."

The Reach towered above us. We were so close.

"C'mon," I said. I put my head down and we scurried towards the Reach.

"How will we get in there? We don't have a contact," said Coyne.

"Let's find a safe place to hide first," I said.

Soon we heard the marching of soldiers echo down the winding streets. We ducked into a side street of little brick shops with apartments above. It was there that I spotted a green weather-beaten sign: The Monkey Tree Haberdashery. There was something familiar about it, and it bore a picture of a monkey puzzle tree like the one at the Cress. I somehow knew it.

"There. I've been there before," I said. "I'm sure of it."

"Go. I'll try to lead them away from you."

"No, I can't lose you too." I grabbed at him, but Coyne pushed me down the street towards the row of shops.

"I'll find you." Then he ran back out the way he came, looking for guards. I heard Raturro squeals—Coyne had lifted his Rat-gah. It was like he wanted to be caught.

I slipped inside the little shop, hoping Coyne would find our friends and bring them back safe.

Inside it was quiet and dimly lit. The walls were a deep purple and the ceiling was low. In the corner, a fat grey

Raturro sat on a well-worn green velvet cushion. She wore a tall, red hat and matching velvet vest with golden tassels. Her eyes were closed, her breathing deep and comforting. I hoped she would sleep awhile as I figured out what to do next. The shop was filled with hats of all styles and shapes; large feathers and colourful flowers decorated them.

I tiptoed through the shop, getting as far away from the door and windows as I could. Out of breath, I hid in a back corner and strained to listen for any sounds from outside, but it was quiet. Too quiet. I tried to steady my breathing, but I was so frightened it seemed like the pounding of my heart could be heard all over Antiica.

On the dust-filled shelves above my head there were several old cameras lined with cobwebs. They were like the antiques I had seen in a shop on Earth. Then I spied a picture much like the one in my pocket. I reached up and grabbed it, wiping the grime off. It was the same picture of my parents and me at the Cress. Suddenly realizing that I wasn't alone, I turned to find the ancient Raturro, now much larger, looming above me.

"Ko-ru-ku?" she whispered.

I lifted the shawl from my face and nodded.

"You are safe, Ko-ru-ku." The rat bowed slightly to me, "I am Virtu of the Deep Nestling Raturro, though I have been a City Raturro now many years."

"Where did you get this?" I pushed the photo towards her. "I have the same one." I reached into my pocket.

"Ah, I took this when you were but a pup. I was the family photographer for many moons, Ko-ru-ku." She smiled at it fondly. "But you are no longer a pup. Where have the years gone?"

"My mother, she's in the Reach. Majellan has her and I need to find a way to free her."

"The Queen, yes, there have been rumours of her capture," she said.

"What are these lines on the back?" I turned my photo over to show her the blue lines.

"Ah, you found my map. I made it for you knowing some day you would return home, Ko-ru-ku. Now you are here and you must use it."

"But how?"

Shouting erupted from out on the street. Was it the Raturro Guard?

"You will soon find out, Ko-ru-ku," said Virtu. She pulled open a door that was hidden behind a stack of hats. "It will take you home."

"Huh?" I peeked inside the room and all I could see were more shelves of hats and a brick wall. Behind us, the front door creaked open and the searchers spilled into the shop. Virtu pushed me inside the room and I heard the door click behind me.

In the blackness, my photograph emitted an eerie blue glow. I ran my hands over the brick wall, scanning for an escape, a door. Nothing. Outside in the shop, I could hear the booming voice of the Raturro Guard.

"The human scent ends here, Keeper. Are you hiding an enemy of the Raturro?" roared a voice.

"I have many customers who come for my hats, Thane Majellan, but I have served no enemies today. Hm, what sort of hat might they purchase?" said Virtu with a flourish. "Tufted velvet with a sloping brim. Perhaps a bright feather?"

"Enough!" shouted Majellan.

Majellan? Here? It wouldn't be long until he found me. I backed against the brick wall willing it to move. *Chimera? Chimera? Are you here?* How could this photo take me home?

The door burst open and suddenly Majellan appeared in front of me. The light from the open door framed me like a spotlight. I was afraid to look, afraid of what he would do to me.

Majellan growled deeply, and his lips pulled back to reveal huge yellowed teeth dripping with saliva. He was immense—a couple feet taller than me and wide as the doorway. As he drew closer I could hear his heavy, panting breath, and feel its heat near my face. Any thought of negotiating peace with him quickly vanished from my thoughts. I shut my eyes, expecting the worst.

It was suddenly quiet, and when I finally found the courage I peeked open one eye to find a filmy blue light floating in front of me. Majellan was still inches away from me, his long whiskers probing the air, his ears twitching and turning—but he couldn't see me. Frozen in place, barely breathing, I was afraid if I moved the protective blue light would disappear.

Majellan paced the room like a caged animal. He swept shelves full of hats to the ground, roaring in disappointment before slamming the door behind him as he left. His terrifying presence stayed in the room long after he'd gone.

For what seemed like an age, I stood alone in the dark waiting for Virtu to come and tell me it was okay to come out. But it was too quiet, and I realized Majellan must have taken her. How did he find me so quickly? I guessed the oil had worn off and my scent had led him to me.

My photograph illuminated the room. I tried to edge forward towards the door, but I was stuck. I couldn't move ahead. I turned. Behind me appeared a tunnel dug out of the dirt and clay foundation of the building.

"Chimera?" I whispered, wondering if it had something to do with the magic, but only my voice echoed back. I shone the light farther down the dark tunnel and it seemed to go on for a long, long way. I needed answers; I needed to find my Mom, so I followed the glowing map down the tunnel and hoped that the light would last.

Chapter Seventeen

The tunnel went on forever. The photo lit my way, but I was worried it might fade out and leave me in darkness. At times I had to crawl and bumped the head of the Rat-gah as the tunnel narrowed. My hands felt unremarkable dirt and clay turn to stone and I ran my fingers over ribbons of colourful rock. I scurried up the steeply sloping tunnel, desperate to find Mom. Coyne would find Mercy and the others, I assured myself. We'd meet back at the Cress if we were split up. That was the plan.

Right now, I was just another rat in the Reach.

The photo faded, casting shadows over wooden crates filled with bottles and jars, sacks of roots and old, stacked up furniture. In the middle of a cellar, the blue line stopped dead. Wooden stairs led to a door. The light seeping under the doorway ahead made me hesitate.

The tunnel had sealed behind me, blocking my escape. My fate was being decided by the photograph. I crept up the stairs and pushed, but the old wooden door wouldn't budge. No latch. No lock. Underneath, I glimpsed a speckled tiled floor and wondered if it was a Raturro house. I took a chance and knocked.

Nothing.

I knocked harder.

Shuffling feet on the floor.

The hair on my neck bristled.

The door swung open and I was faced with a huge, grey Raturro in a long brown dress made of coarse thread. She was much taller and wider than the Deep Nestling Raturro, but she also looked friendly. She wore cracked spectacles and her white-streaked nose constantly twitched.

"I need your help," I said. "I came through the tunnel."

"Tunnel? There's no tunnel down there, pup." She gazed past me, bewildered, then sniffed me suspiciously. "Oh, you gave me a fright. I thought for a moment you were a human child. Musty cellar! Well, you'd better come and get warm by the fire. Have you eaten?"

"Uh, no," I said, following as she shuffled into the kitchen where a roaring fire awaited. But she stopped midstride, turned around. Sniff. Sniff.

"Am I in the Reach?"

"Yes, pup."

"Thane's Reach? Right inside it?"

"Well, of course. This is the gardener's cottage. My husband and I tend Thane Majellan's garden."

I dashed to the tiny window and peeked out. Even in the dark, I could make out the Reach towering above me, and near its tip, lights on in the round windows. I'd made it!

"Are you from Deep Nestling by chance?" Sniff. Sniff. She came towards me.

"I've been to Deep Nestling." I admitted. "Do you know Shale?"

She thought for a moment. "Well, there's a name I haven't heard in a long time. My pups went to school with a Deep Nestling Raturro called Shale. It was a strange time. The Thane decreed that Raturro would attend schools with the humans, and my daughter, Brill, was in the first class to mix. What an adventure that was!"

"School?" I exclaimed. "Did you know—" but I paused, unsure if I should continue.

"Know who, pup?"

"The Thane or the Queen?"

"As a matter of fact, I did." She smiled warmly. "Brill would bring them both home for study sessions. A big group of them—they talked about what they could become in the future. It was a special time. We were all different then."

"You were? Different how?" I pressed.

"Well, this world you see now, so full of hatred and war, it wasn't always like this. There was a time when Raturro were free, and I'm not talking about the First Raturro..."

"The first? What do you mean?"

She ignored my question and dove into her memories, "Brill was in the graduating class that year—oh, it was exciting. But a bit dangerous. You see, all the uproar caused by the decision to place Raturro in the schools was lost on them. But through it, we finally got to know humans, up close."

"Is it true Jaagar and Majellan were once friends?" I remembered what Coyne had said.

"Oh, Majellan was loved by many, including the humans. He was charismatic, bit of a rogue, but you could see he was a born leader. But the scandal over the Queen was what—"

"What scandal? What happened?"

"Oh, you're just a pup. You're far too young to hear about—"

"What?"

"Well, it was just a rumour—they were very close friends, nothing more—used to go everywhere together, but young Jaag had a temper. Accused Majellan of trying to steal his girl, and from then on Majellan and Jaag were always fighting." She moved to the stove and reached for a bowl.

"But my mother hates rats." I couldn't process the possibility that Mom had been best friends with a Raturro—especially Majellan.

"Your mother?" She examined me more closely. "Who are you?" She sniffed me again.

"I am a human." I pushed the Rat-gah back to reveal my face.

"It can't be!" She stuttered and the blue earthenware bowl she held crashed to pieces on the tiled floor. "Let me look at you." She dusted off her spectacles to inspect me. "What on Antiica?" she exclaimed. "There's nary a human family left in the land. It seems you're quite lost, my dear. Quite lost." Sitting down at the kitchen table, she dabbed at her eyes with her burlap sleeve.

"I'm sorry about your bowl," I said, picking up the broken shards.

"Oh, no, it's not that. I was just remembering a happier time when life here was full of friends—humans and Raturro. Now…" her voice faltered. "Oh, where are my manners. I'm Dima."

"I'm Kyra Murch, and I've come here to—"

"It's true then. What they're saying? It's true?"

"I don't know what they're saying," I said.

"They say you destroyed a human village and freed the Raturro slaves."

"Me? Well, no, not exactly...."

"They say you stood up in front of the entire village and declared yourself Queen of the Realm."

"What?"

"You're here to kill Majellan, aren't you?"

"Kill him? No!"

"Sounds like the perfect revenge plot to me." Dima got up and went to the window. "Where's your army? Are they outside the Reach? Are we being invaded?" she asked worriedly.

"Um, no. It's just me."

"Oh, well then." Her nose twitched. "You'll have time for some tea." Dima stifled a smile as she shuffled absentmindedly with a teapot in her paw, searching for the tea.

A door opened in the next room. Was it Majellan? Was this a trap? I pulled the Rat-gah over my face.

"That's my husband, Cheam," said Dima. "Wait 'til he hears about the invasion!"

"There's no invasion," I said.

"Invasion? Who're you talking to, Dima?" said Cheam as he shuffled into the kitchen. "You'll never guess what happened in the market today—"

"We have a guest, Cheam," said Dima.

Would he run out and call the guards? I pulled back the Rat-gah.

He, too, was a tall City Raturro, but seemed just as ancient and confused as Dima. He stared at me and rubbed a tuft of thick white fur on the top of his head.

"It's the human child. *The Last Murch*!" she said.

"There's not been a Murch in Thane's Reach for years," Cheam said casually, stepping forward to accept a frothy drink from his wife.

"Kyra Murch." I offered him my hand. "I'm here to save my mother. She's imprisoned in the Reach."

He stared at me then back at Dima.

"The Queen is here?" Dima nearly dropped the pitcher of drink. "This is terrible," said Dima. "War is a terrible business."

"Then you're the princess," Cheam said as he sat down at the table, his nose sniffing the air. He pulled at the long white hairs on his chin.

"It's Kyra," I said, sniffing the Rat-gah. Was the oil wearing off again? "I've got to get inside."

"If we're caught with this human," said Cheam, exchanging a nervous glance with his wife, "that's treason."

"Oh, she's just a pup looking for her mother," said Dima. "I sometimes think the rebels are no different than the humans. Majellan is taxing us, taking everything, and locking up Raturro for no reason. He was supposed to be our saviour. If I'd known they've been keeping that good woman right outside our door...."

I was so close to Mom, I could feel it.

"We'll have to get her into the dungeon," said Cheam. "It's the only way it will work."

"The way what'll work?" I asked confused.

"The rebellion. We got us another rebellion, Dima." He jumped up and did a little jig, and then his face went all serious. "Of course, the last thing we want is Majellan to find you. There's no telling what he'll do if he does. He's got everyone scared," Cheam continued. "He thinks everyone's a spy. Everything's a conspiracy." He held up a crooked paw for emphasis. "If you cross him, he'll rip out your claws and shame you in front of all. Or worse." He drew a line across his wizened throat with his claw.

"Oh, no! Do you know if Majellan has captured my friends? They were in the market."

"There haven't been any other humans here," said Cheam.

"My friends are Raturro," I said, "from Deep Nestling, and, well, a boy from the Plains."

Cheam brightened up, "Ah, Deep Nestling is starting a rebellion!"

"No!"

"I'm sorry. We don't see much going on around here. Dima and I are in the garden mostly. We're not rebels."

"Look, I'm not here to start any rebellion. It's not an invasion. You don't have to do anything except get me inside," I pleaded. "I promise I'll never tell how I got in. All I need are directions to where they could be holding my mom. And the safest way to get her out."

"Hm. There's a lot of cells down in the dungeons. But there's lots of places up high she could be. In a tower, someplace like that. But no one's said anything. There's been no mention of a special guest at the Reach. And the cells are full."

"Full? Of humans?"

Cheam's face went serious, sad. "Those cells are full of Raturro."

"Why don't you go back to the kitchen and ask around?" said Dima. "See if they're preparing anything special."

"No, I'm not sure we can trust any of those kitchen boys. Some of them are related to Majellan. But it's late; they'll all be nested by now," he said.

"We're all related to Majellan," Dima tittered.

"I need to go now," I said, pacing towards the door.

Dima and Cheam were alarmed. "Oh, no, you can't just wander through the Reach. There's rebels everywhere," said Cheam.

"It's nighttime. Won't they all be asleep?" I asked and immediately felt silly. War never sleeps.

"We could get you in through the kitchen." He hesitated. "Then you'd be on your own, little princess."

"She will not! You'll go with her and help her, you old cod," said Dima.

"We can't turn against our kind, Dima!" he sputtered.

"She just wants her mother," pleaded Dima. "Is that too much to ask?"

"No, it's better if I go alone," I said. But Dima glared at us both over her cracked spectacles and we knew she was right.

"One of these might open the prison cells," Cheam said, emptying out a wooden boxful of ancient rusty keys. He grabbed a few of the largest keys and two long metal tools like chopsticks. "These've gotten me into a few secret places in my time." He winked. "Ah, and there's a few tunnels under the Reach. I've never been down them, but one of 'em should lead out under the wall. Unless Majellan blocked them up." He scratched inside his ear with one of the tools.

Dima tucked my shawl around my neck, leaving a gap that made it easier for me to see out of the Rat-gah. I held a small basket of food and stooped over so that I'd look like Dima. In the darkness of night I still appeared a Raturro, but I wasn't sure if the oil was still working. I would have to risk it.

Dima hugged me hard before pushing us out the door like she was sending us to market for some bread. "Off you go!"

We crept through a wide cobblestoned courtyard towards the kitchen entrance. No sign of any guards. Inside the massive kitchen, we found a fire lit in the stove and a pot of something bubbling on top. Cheam's paw trembled and his claws clicked on the metal latch of the door. But he led me through and we were quickly out of the kitchen.

The light in the hallway was dim. We soon came to an immense marble-clad room filled with elegant antique furniture and thick colourful rugs. The grand entranceway took my breath away. I had been there before.

"This is where the Thane's lodgings begin. Come," Cheam whispered.

A wide, white marble staircase inlaid with dark onyx and pale green jade led up to the Thane's rooms. A jolt of memory went through me. I had run up and down those stairs sometime in the past. I wanted to pull off my shoes and feel the cool marble on my toes, but Cheam's heavy paw on my arm reminded me to keep up.

We followed another hallway, taking the stairs down into darkness. As we went deeper into the bowels of the Reach, I shivered in the frigid air. A strange sensation was building up inside of me. It was how I felt when the chimera was near. I paused and pulled my hand out of the Rat-gah, then placed it on a creamy limestone column.

Chimera?

Nothing. Just cold emptiness.

We came out of the stairwell and into a dark hallway. Suddenly, two immense Raturro guards lumbered towards us.

"You're working late again, Tor," said Cheam heartily. The taller of the guards nodded and glanced over at me. Even though I couldn't see all of him, he loomed above me and was the biggest Raturro I'd ever encountered, even bigger than Majellan. He must have been seven feet tall, not including his ears.

"Dima's not so well, but we were told to bring some food for our special guest." Cheam clucked at Tor.

Tor and the other guard nodded and walked on. Then we heard them stop behind us. Tor's immense nose snorted and sniffed. "Odd," he said. "That stench?"

Cheam gave a cough and answered, "It's my chest poultice—a balm for my aching lungs."

Tor and his companion continued to sniff and snort but kept walking.

"There will be more guards ahead, princess," whispered Cheam as we continued down the long hallway.

"Call me Kyra," I said. Soon we came to a junction and paused as voices echoed down the hallway towards us. I slipped the scarf down and lifted the Rat-gah up so I could see his face.

"Sounds like there's quite a few guards down there," said Cheam, his whiskers twitching nervously.

"You're doing fine," I assured him.

"What if it doesn't work? They might want to inspect the food—and you," he said. Was the old rat losing his nerve?

"It's not too late to go home," I said, worried what might happen if he got caught.

"No, pup. Dima'd have my whiskers on a shelf. I'm with you all the way," he whispered, a twinkle in his watery eye. The grip of his paw on my arm was strong. "No matter what happens to me, just make sure that the Queen is saved and my Dima's not harmed."

Tucked back in my Rat-gah, I followed Cheam to the main prison gate. "What is it, old one?" a fat Raturro guard barked at us. Two of them sat at a table casually throwing some small square game tiles between them. They didn't bother getting up.

"We've come with the food Majellan ordered," Cheam answered, his voice unswerving.

"Food?"

"For the special guest," Cheam said, clucking at the guard.

The guard's eyes were upon me, and I managed a sickly cough.

"Dima's not too well down here in the cold," said Cheam impatiently, and then I heard the rustle of keys. The guard finally heaved himself up out of his chair.

"Don't be long and don't speak to anyone," ordered the guard as he swung open the heavy, iron gate. "Down to the far end of the corridor and turn left, then left again."

CLANK! The door shut loudly behind us and the lock turned.

We were in. Cheam and I shared a relieved sigh then I was hit with a wall of wet air and the buzz of hundreds of voices. Moans and wails mostly, but whispers too.

As we walked down a long row of cells, we passed sick and tortured Raturro of all sizes and colours. They were jammed into the small cells. Some whined and cried. Others just lay in a ball of fur in the corner of their cells. Cheam let out a guttural whimper as he witnessed the horror around us. I took his arm and urged him down the hallway hoping to get the grisly sight past us, but the halls were long and branched off many times.

I whispered to Cheam, "Which way?"

He came to his senses, grabbed a roll of bread out of the basket and approached a sad Raturro whose clawless, emaciated paws stuck out through the bars of the cell. They whispered a moment as Cheam slipped him the bread, then with renewed vigor Cheam took my arm.

We turned left into the hallway but still had no sign of her. My pace quickened, and my back straightened. Cheam huffed a few paces behind. The buzz of prisoners grew louder as news of the bread exchange—and the aroma, I figured—spread fast. Paws grasped at us as we ran past.

"Mom!" I half-whispered, half-shouted, rounding the corner looking for her. I lifted the Rat-gah from my face. "Mom?"

"Kyra?" Mom's weak voice echoed through the cells.

I followed her voice. When I turned another corner, there she was, lying on the dirt floor of a dark cell.

"Mom!"

"Kyra! What are you doing here?" She pulled herself up the bars of her cage and into the dim light. One arm hung broken and useless at her side. Her face bore the scabbed-over slash marks from Majellan's claws, but she had a defiant look in her eyes. She grabbed me and hugged me through the cage. Even with the cold bars between us, it was the best hug of my life.

"Oh, Mom, I was so afraid I'd never see you again," I whispered.

Cheam bowed low and then pulled out the stack of keys and tools and set to work on opening the cell.

"Hurry!" I said to Cheam.

Mom pulled out of the embrace and her hand went to my wrist.

"Kyra, where's the bracelet? Put it back on."

"Uh...."

"You don't have it?" She looked horrified.

"I'm sorry, but the Corvie sort of have it."

"The Corvie?!"

"It's a long story."

"How did you get here?"

"Dad found me first. He's alive. I was in the Armory and then I fell through the chimera, kind of, and I came looking for you."

"Okay," Mom said, taking it all in. "What's the plan? Are there others with you?"

"The plan has been, er, changing. I figured you would know the Reach better than anyone," I said. She looked at me in disbelief as I hit her with a barrage of questions. "Where are the secret tunnels? Can they take us out of here? Do you know if there were any other prisoners brought here today? My friends—I need to know they're safe. Have you seen them?"

"You came here without a plan to get us out?" she said, finally understanding.

Click. Pop. The cell door swung open. She was free. I wrapped my arms around her and gave her another hug. She winced, the pain in her arm too much.

"I'm the only one down here, Kyra. I haven't seen any humans in the Reach."

"But, Mom, we have to find them," I said.

She shook her head, no. "We have to get you out of here." She shared an angry look with Cheam as if blaming him for my crazy rescue, but she held her tongue. "This way," she pointed to a darkened hallway.

"We came in through the kitchen, Ma'am," whispered Cheam. "If we can get back there, then we're home free."

"No. This way. We can access the tunnels."

"Hurry!" I said.

Mom took the lead, and Cheam and I ran down the hallway away from her cell, her home for the past week or however long I'd been on Antiica. Soon the hallway grew darker and the buzz of the pitiful prisoners faded behind us. When we came to another heavy iron door, Cheam expertly popped the lock open with his tools. I squeezed Mom's hand as we came out into a well-lit, empty hallway.

Cheam sniffed the air. "The guards are everywhere."

"Can you lock it again?" I asked.

"No time," said Mom. "This way. It leads to our old quarters." She ran across the hall and up a rough-hewn staircase lit with torches.

I paused. "What about the tunnels?"

But Mom had a determined look in her eye. "No, there's something I must find first."

"Mom, we have to get out of here before the guards find us," I warned. "Before Majellan knows we're here."

She turned to me, unwavering. "We have an opportunity here. If we can find where Majellan keeps the plans for his next attack, we could save many human lives."

"Er, the longer we stay in the castle, the more chance we have of getting caught," Cheam whispered.

"Then go, Cheam," said Mom.

"Ah, you remember me."

"Yes, Brill's father. Your kindness shall be repaid," she said warmly. Then Mom darted upstairs and we had no choice but to follow her. We climbed another two levels, through a rusty iron and wood door only to be hit on the face by a heavy fabric.

I froze, tried to get my bearings. We were behind a large tapestry concealing the door. We crept out and found ourselves in a long hallway outside a series of doors. Heavy wooden chairs and a small table nestled under a nearby window, and a half-empty mug of something sat on the table. As we passed, I reached out and grasped it. It was warm. Maybe we were a little too close to Majellan.

I glanced out a window and saw guards in the courtyard below, but they didn't look alarmed. Yet. Mom listened a moment before opening the nearest door.

Inside was a small but regal sitting room with a rich purple carpet and matching couch and chair. I had been there before, remembered sitting at the fireplace drying my hair as Mom pulled a silver brush through it. The mantle was covered in vases and ornaments, every one of them held a story.

Mom had a look of longing on her face. She missed her old home. We crept to the next door and listened again. Inside was Dad's office and sitting room where people visited him, sought his advice. I would run in to say goodnight and jump onto his lap. He'd embrace me, kiss me on the cheek, then send me back to Mom's waiting arms.

Mom rushed to a large desk filled with maps and plans. She glanced over the documents, shuffling them, searching.

"Someone's coming." Cheam's nose went up, his ears twitched, but Mom ignored him and continued to shuffle through the papers. At last, she found what she was looking for. She quickly read a document, then with a worried look put it back where she'd found it.

"This is worse than I thought," she murmured.

One last look around the room and we all dashed out with Cheam leading the way.

As we crept back towards the tapestry, a flash of heat went through me—blinding pain hit my head. *Chimera?*

When Mom pulled back the tapestry, we came face to face with Majellan and two huge guards.

And he laughed. "Seize them!" roared Majellan. I tried to run but Majellan grabbed me first. He was massive, strong and his muscular arms easily held me tightly. "A pup, that's all you are."

With only one good arm, Mom was no match for the guard but she fought ferociously.

"Perhaps now you'll tell me where Jaagar's stronghold is located? Where is the One Stone?" growled Majellan.

Mom turned on him. "Don't touch her, Majellan. She's not part of your war!"

"My war?" barked Majellan. "You stole all the land from the Raturro and enslaved us. You started the fight, and I'm going to finish it even if I have to wipe out every last one of you. Where's Jaagar hiding? The Stone is mine!"

"It belongs to the crown!" said Mom.

Another guard had captured Cheam. "Traitor!" I heard him say as he lashed Cheam with a whip.

"No! Stop!" I shrieked, trying to pull away from Majellan's grasp.

"When the army comes, they will have no mercy on you, Majellan. Jaagar will destroy the entire Raturro race and there's nothing you can do to stop him," she said, her eyes alight.

My mouth hung open. I'd never heard her talk like that. She was the sweet mom who was understanding and rarely ever yelled at me. She took me shopping and bought me pizza and ice cream and listened to my problems at school. She sang me to sleep. Did I really know her?

The answer chilled me to the bone.

"Let us both go and your people will be spared," she bargained. "We'll work on a peace treaty, abolish slavery. We'll find a solution." Mom suddenly softened, entreated him. "Maji, please."

Majellan was startled for a moment, then regained his composure. "Enough, Rikki," Majellan snorted, but they were once friends. He brushed away the feeling. "Your time for treaties is over. There will be no mercy for you or Jaag."

Mom drew in a sharp breath. "Oh, Maji. You're going to regret this."

"We're past regrets," he said, and I sensed it had a deeper meaning.

Majellan grabbed my arms with his large paws and pulled back each of my sleeves, exposing my bare wrists. A look of surprise crossed his face. "It looks like the little Stone Traveller is lost. Did you forget your jewels? Take the child and throw her into the deepest, darkest prison cell."

"I'm not a child!" I roared back, kicking him in his hairy shins.

He pushed me towards Tor and two new Raturro guards who had joined us.

"Mom! Mom!" I screamed as they dragged me away from her. But she wasn't finished with Majellan. She gave him a bitter stare, as if willing him to die. And in that moment all of my hopes and dreams fizzled away. I had risked the life of my friends for a war I didn't understand. For parents I didn't even know. And now there was no way out.

CHAPTER EIGHTEEN

There was a lump on the back of my head. Swollen and bloody, it pulsed and throbbed. Every time I moved it seemed like the pain grew and grew. I was alone in a cell. Where was Mom? Had I put her in even greater danger?

I couldn't let Majellan win.

The Raturro had taken my Rat-gah, but left me with my own clothes. I had promised to return it to Deep Nestling. It was sacred. How could I ever face Brae again? I fished in my pocket and found the photo and stared at the image of my once-perfect family. My only hope was that Coyne and the others had escaped. Majellan would show them no mercy. After the odd exchange between Mom and Majellan, maybe I'd just imagined they were more than friends.

I willed the ridiculous thought out of my head. What had Mercy said about concentrating hard to contact the chimera?

"Chimera, can you hear me? I need your help." I crawled over to lay my hand on the wall, searching, hoping. Granite, a coarse, enduring rock—the stuff mountains were made of. Solid. Built to last. Eternal.

"Chimera, please!" The stone was cold and unforgiving as I closed my eyes, slumped against it. The chimera was gone. My friends were gone. Mom was gone. I had failed and was completely on my own.

The iron doors of my cell creaked open. Two Raturro guards pulled me to my feet and half-dragged me along the corridor. I glanced into the empty cells, relieved, hoping that meant my friends were hiding somewhere safe.

We scurried along at a swift pace. My arms ached from their terrible grip. Soon we were met by the strong stench of animals and laughter. Raturro laughter. But it wasn't soft and joyful like Deep Nestling, it was deep and hateful.

A door was flung open and the guards pushed me forward. I emerged onto the balcony of an open-air arena set in the centre of the Reach. The seats were full of thousands of Raturro in all shapes and sizes. They chattered and feasted, excitedly waiting for something to happen. A wave of memory crashed over me of Mom, Dad, and I sitting on this very balcony, laughing and enjoying a show. The memory quickly faded.

Sensing I was not alone, I turned to find Majellan sitting behind me at a long food-filled table. I was alarmed to see Mercy by his side, her face pained like she was still a slave in the market. One of her paws was wrapped in a blood-soaked rag. Had Majellan tortured her? I fought back the rising lump in my throat. I would not let Majellan see me cry. Mercy stifled her relief when she saw me, and the slave girl disappeared; she sat taller.

"Sit," he ordered.

"Never," I replied with as much force as I could muster. My thoughts of peace had disappeared and I was dismayed to find how easily I hated Majellan.

He laughed and stuffed a meaty bone into his ugly, fanged mouth. "You're just like your father, Murchling. He barks but has no bite. And where is the coward now? He sent a pup to do a Thane's work?" Majellan's voice echoed across the crowd and they erupted in cackles and barks.

"He didn't send me."

"Really?" he mocked. "Aren't you his secret weapon?" Majellan had the crowd's attention now. He was putting on a show.

"Where's my mom?"

"You're about to join her."

Mercy squeaked as a burly guard pushed Lody, Scat, Gnarls, and Peep onto the balcony. I was so relieved to see them alive.

"Not much of an army you brought with you," Majellan joked. "I don't see how you could bring us down with a band of Nestling pups." His onlookers laughed and guffawed. "But thank you for bringing them. The Deep Nestling Raturro are renowned for their entertainment value." He clapped his greasy paws together. "Let's have a show! We must celebrate! The war is over. The Raturro have won!"

A deafening cheer erupted from the crowd. "Long live the Raturro! Long live the Raturro!" Majellan waved, egging them on.

"I have the Queen and the Princess. Your father has no choice but to surrender to me," Majellan declared.

"Never!" I screamed.

The guard pulled Lody forward, instructing her to sing. Her voice was hoarse at first, tight with fear, but when she closed her tear-filled eyes it became smooth and melodic. Scat and the twins started to hop and dance but their acrobatic show felt forced and fearful.

Majellan tapped a razor-sharp claw on the wooden table, keeping time. "I don't suppose you've even discovered the chimera's secrets, have you, little one? Or else you would have been here and gone without my noticing. Such a tragedy. Even the once infallible Stone Travellers have fallen by the wayside." He tittered. "Did you know you were the human race's last chance? And you failed. So much for the prophecy!" Majellan's laugh was full of menace. Then it faded to a sneer. "All I want to know is where your father and his army are hiding, Murchling. I know they can't be too far. He has something that belongs to me, to all Raturro. The One Stone."

The Raturro crowd cheered.

"The One Stone must be returned," he said.

Was he talking about the Adularia stone? The one under the dryer in the laundry room back home? I shook my head; I would never reveal its location. "I haven't heard of it, and I have no idea where he is."

"Come on, Murchling. Surely you want to save your own life? Are you a human or a mouse?"

"Don't call me that!"

"You're so like Aerikka when she was your age. So blind. We were all friends at one time, brothers and sisters. Hard to believe I ever called Jaagar an ally. But I have a soft spot for you. You've inherited your family's tawdry mess. If you tell me where he is, I'll let you go. You can walk out of the Reach right now and go wherever you like. Free."

"I don't know where he is," I repeated. It was true. Sort of. The Armory was deep in a mountain someplace. But not impossible to find with the Raturro's keen sense of smell.

In an instant, Majellan dove at me, wrapped his razor-sharp claws around my throat, drawing blood. "Tell me!" I tried to push him away, but it was no use. He was too big, too strong. I struggled for breath.

"No, Majellan, please spare her," cried Mercy.

"Would you like to take her place, cousin?" Majellan dropped me on the cold marble floor. "This is spoiling my dinner," he laughed. Then he shouted to his guards, "Let the fun begin. Take her to the arena!"

As I was dragged away, I met Mercy's worried eyes.

I was pulled down a flight of rough stone steps, thrown through a wooden door, and landed on the arena's prickly sawdust floor. I lay sprawled on my back staring at the dark, angry sky above me. The arena was oval-shaped, with a high cement wall and a number of closed doors around the perimeter. At the end was a set of tall, arched double doors. Majellan stared down at me from the balcony, Mercy at his side.

"It's your last chance, Murchling. Tell me where I can find your father and the One Stone or you'll suffer the consequences," he threatened.

I stood on unsteady legs, defiant. I would reveal no secrets.

A lock turned, a door flew open, and out came Cheam, battered and barely able to stand, but alive. And then Mom was pushed through another door. I ran to throw my arms around her. She held me tightly with her good arm.

"Oh, Kyra, my baby, what have they done to you?" she said, seeing the bloody claw marks around my neck. Then she turned to the balcony. "Don't you ever put another claw on my daughter, Majellan." Mom ordered, her voice deep and commanding. "Let her go. She has no idea where the stronghold is. Even I was never allowed to know."

"Where did you get that haughtiness from?" Majellan laughed. "Your family were peasants and you rooted your way into the royal family like a plague."

Another door clicked. It was Coyne.

"Coyne!" I ran to him. He was bruised and had lost his Rat-gah, but he was okay. His eyes lit up and he wrapped his arms around me.

"Kyra!"

"We have to get out of here," I whispered.

"Yeah, but how?"

"There's got to be a way." I gripped his hand and he squeezed it tightly.

"Let's see if this changes your mind." Majellan waved to a guard and the arena doors creaked open.

An unearthly screech came from the darkness. Coyne and I stood watching, frozen in place.

And then I saw it.

RAWK!

It was the Corvie. The missing Corvie!

Mom reeled. "Oh, no! How on Earth did they get a Corvie?"

I glanced up at the balcony and caught Mercy's eye.

"No, Majellan! She's the Last Murch!" shouted Mercy above the jeering crowd. "She will save us all."

"I have already saved the Raturro, cousin," laughed Majellan.

I elbowed Coyne. "Follow my lead."

"What?" he said.

RAWK!

The Corvie, weighted down by heavy chains around its legs, teetered out of its holding cell. A lanky Raturro cracked a whip behind it, forcing it forward. The Corvie was confused, weak, starved: it had been hidden away in the dark where its flock could never find it. And we were its next meal.

"What're you doing, Kyra?" Mom asked as I moved slowly towards Cheam, trying not to call attention to us.

I met Cheam's gaze. "If it comes for you," I warned him, "bow down as low as you can go. Understand? I'm going to get us all out of here, but I need you to protect Mom."

Cheam nodded, excited. "Are you going to kill the Corvie with your bare hands, pup?"

"Kill it? No, I'm going to free it."

Majellan laughed, delighted at turning his enemies into a nice light snack for the Corvie. But I would not let him win. I took a deep breath and ran towards the Corvie with all my might.

"Kyra!" Mom shouted after me.

The Corvie was coming to its senses. It quickly spotted me and pulled at the heavy rope tether attached to its legs. The Raturro guard slowly let out the tether allowing it closer and closer to me.

"Majellan, stop this before someone gets seriously hurt," Mom shouted.

Majellan snorted. "Hurt? Let's hope so!"

Huffing and puffing came from behind me. I wasn't alone. Cheam was gaining on me. I don't know where he got the strength to run at all. Then Coyne was on my other side.

"You might have told me what you were thinking," said Coyne.

"Did you have a better idea?"

"Feed the Corvie!" Majellan roared behind us.

"Feed the Corvie!" The crowd chanted. "Feed. The. Corvie!"

The hungry Corvie staggered towards us as its tether was loosened. The bird was smaller than the ones we'd encountered on the mountaintop, but still big enough to make a meal out of us. The Corvie set its sights on me and lurched forward again.

One of the Corvie's eyes was red and swollen so I pointed Cheam towards its blind side, but he had his own plans. Cheam banked to the left and the Corvie staggered towards him as I circled around to its right.

Guards hollered above us, but I trained my eyes on the great bird. I ducked under the Corvie's wing as it fluttered past me and managed to grab one of its ropes. The Corvie sensed me right away and swung its head around to peck me with its beak. Then Cheam let out a squeak and the Corvie was after him once more.

Coyne rolled under the bird and jumped up beside me. He had figured out my plan.

"Kyra, no!" called Mom from the other side of the arena. Suddenly the Corvie's beak stabbed me on the back of the leg. The pain shot through me like a dagger. Coyne dove on me and we rolled out of reach.

The scent of fresh blood sent the Corvie into a tailspin. It thrashed wildly about, stabbing at the ground again and again. But Cheam pulled the Corvie's attention again.

"We have to free it," I shouted. Coyne grabbed at the tether, tried to undo it.

The Corvie's tail feathers were coarse and thick. I clutched them and scrambled onto its back. It jumped and jerked like a bucking bronco, but I held on with all my might.

"Ko-ru-ku. Ko-ru-ku!" I shrieked, but my words had no effect.

"It can't hold us all!" Coyne said.

"Guards!" Majellan's commanding voice boomed through the arena. More guards joined in to pull at the Corvie's tether, but they were too fearful of the bird to come after me.

"I'm here, you mangy bird. Come get your dinner," Cheam laughed. I liked that old rat.

The Corvie swerved towards Cheam, and I lost my balance. I was hanging on by just a few feathers and suddenly too exhausted to pull myself back up. The angry Corvie flapped its wings, rising off the ground then falling back down. Between the Corvie's lift-offs, I could see it gaining on Cheam. I needed to pull myself up higher to get to its neck to control it.

"Coyne?" I yelled.

Under the moving bird, Coyne wrestled with the tether. "Almost there," he shouted back, keeping one eye on the Raturro guard at the end of the Corvie's rope.

"Ko-ru-ku! Ko-ru-ku!" I called, but the bird was blind with hunger. Finally, Cheam stopped and faced the bird.

"No, Cheam! Get down!" I shouted, but he stood his ground. In a flash the Corvie was on him, stabbing its great beak into Cheam's chest and pinning him down on the ground. With all my strength I lifted myself hand over hand, up the Corvie's back to its neck. Gripping a handful of black feathers on each side of its head, I pulled with all my might.

"Ko-ru-ku!"

The Corvie lifted its beak and cawed loudly, but it was too late. Cheam lay lifeless below us.

"Cheam! Cheam!" I called, but he never moved, never answered. "Nooo!"

Seething with rage, I pulled the Corvie's feathers again. Tears blinded me—I had let Cheam down. I had let Dima down. But I was determined to keep going. It was the only option left.

"Kyra! You're free!" Coyne called, and then I was up in the air. We were flying! We soared up and up, and circled around and around the arena. Below, the guards were running around, confused, Majellan barking orders at them from the balcony. When I leaned forward on the Corvie's neck, it soared down towards the floor of the arena. Coyne was stooped over Cheam, shaking him, but his expression said it was too late. Coyne looked up at me, shook his head.

My anger at Cheam's death gave me strength to pull hard on the bird's neck feathers and I was able to steer it towards the balcony. No one else would die today. "Run," I shouted to my friends. Mercy, Lody, Scat, Peep, and Gnarls jumped and cheered as I flew by. "Run!" I screamed.

Mom stood in the middle of the arena never taking her eyes off me. When our eyes met, she grinned with pride as I banked and directed the great bird towards a panicked Majellan. It was chaos as his guards fled and Raturro ran from the stands in all directions.

In a few wing beats, we were above the balcony. As Majellan reached into his jerkin for a weapon, Mercy grabbed a huge silver jug and threw it at him. The jug bounced off his head splashing purple liquid on his fur. With one push of his strong arms, she went crashing over the edge of the arena and lay still on the sawdust floor.

"Mercy!" I screamed, but she didn't move. No, not Mercy too! As I pulled the Corvie higher up into the air, Coyne was running to her.

The Corvie was getting weaker, unmanageable. We flew haphazardly towards Majellan, but we were slowing and I could barely hold on.

Majellan was now the only Raturro left on the balcony. He stood, defiant, and pulled an oval stone out of his jerkin. As he pointed it at the wall, a bright light flashed and a portal opened.

"Until next time, Murchling!" He grinned slyly and dashed through the light before we could reach him. The stone was just like the one Shale had—the Adularia stone. So that was how Majellan captured Mom, how he got to Earth. He could travel through stone too! He had a portal and could go anywhere he pleased.

The Corvie swerved, soaring upwards trying to escape, but it couldn't make it over the top of the arena. A new wave of Raturro guards stormed into the arena. Something whacked the Corvie on the head and it jerked to one side and lost altitude. We spun wildly out of control down to the sawdust floor where I tumbled head first into the dirt. The Corvie rolled and landed on top of me crushing the breath out of me. Then it hopped up and ran amok around me, flapping its powerful wings, pushing up clouds of dust and feathers.

As I blindly clawed my way to my knees, blood dripped into my eyes from a wound on my head.

RAWK!

The Corvie loomed above me, its one eye red and bloody. The black feathers were ruffled and dusty, making it even more monstrous. As its giant beak was poised in the air above me, I grasped in my pocket for something, anything that would distract the bird. All I found was my photograph, but it was enough. The photograph lit up and I shone its blue light at the great bird. Momentarily distracted by the light, I sacrificed the photo and rolled away. The half-blind Corvie pecked at the photo, cawing loudly in confusion and delight.

The arena suddenly darkened as if the sky had become night. As I scrambled up to my feet, I peered up through the dust and the dark sky became the outline of a hundred massive Corvie.

"RAWK!" boomed Eebon from above. It worked! I had hoped that if I freed the Corvie Eebon would come.

The young Corvie heeded the call and turned to its family. "Rawk," it answered weakly.

"Kyra!" Mom ran to my side and pulled me away from the Corvie, even though I knew the danger had passed.

"It's okay," I said. "The Corvie are our friends."

Out of the dust, Coyne emerged carrying an unconscious Mercy. My heart sank. "Mercy!"

But Coyne grinned as Mercy's big brown eyes fluttered open and a huge sense of relief went through me. She was okay. My friends were safe. I ran to them and pulled them both to me; my heart finally stopped its loud thudding.

Suddenly Eebon's black beak hit the ground beside us. Mom gasped in fear, but I placed my hand on the stony beak. "Eebon!"

"Ko-ru-ku, little one." He turned to Mom and bowed, lowering himself to the ground. "Your Majesty."

Mom was amazed that there was no danger as she nodded back at Eebon.

"Eebon's our friend," I assured her.

"Your debt is paid." Out of Eebon's beak dropped my bracelet. I placed the bracelet back on my wrist where it belonged. Silently, swiftly, the black mass of birds lifted the weak young bird up into the sky. Eebon was the last to leave.

"Wait," I said. "Which one of my friends were you going to keep?"

"It was your heart that needed fixing, Ko-ru-ku." Then Eebon took flight and was gone in moments.

The sun came out from behind the clouds and shone on the almost empty arena. Even Lody, Scat, and the twins had made their escape in the stampede of frightened Raturro.

I ran to Cheam's lifeless body, remembering Shale and how he'd given his life for something he believed in. I lifted Cheam's paw, stroked his fur, and said a silent thank you.

"He was a brave Raturro," Coyne said as he stood beside me. Mercy held onto his arm, steadying herself.

"He was a valiant Raturro," said Mercy.

"He gave his life for us," I whispered.

"Yes, we shall honour him," said Mom, a tear in her eye.

"I should like that," whispered Cheam. He was alive! He opened one eye and clucked his tongue. "I thought that bird'd have my guts for garters. But I've got thicker skin than a serpent!"

"Cheam!" I grabbed him and pulled him into my arms.

"Ouch!" Cheam sputtered.

One of the doors opened and out ran Dima. "Cheam? Cheam?" When she saw that Cheam was injured she sank down beside him and lovingly stroked his face. "You old cod. How'll I get the blood out of that jerkin?"

"Cold water," tittered Cheam.

"Let's get out of here before Majellan returns," Coyne said.

"Dima, you and Cheam need to come with us. Majellan will be looking for you," I said anxiously.

She brushed off my worries. "Go, pup, go. We've been through all this before. It's not the first time I've had to stitch him up."

"Where will you go?" I asked her.

"I'll see you again, my dear. Just don't forget what Cheam has done for you."

"I won't, Dima. He's a hero."

Dima gave me a hug that almost broke my ribs. She was strong, inside and out. Coyne helped Cheam to standing, and he gave a slight bow to Mom and then wrapped an arm around Dima. The two hobbled off towards the end of the arena, and I felt a lump in my throat.

"Thanks," I whispered.

With Mercy between us, Coyne and I moved gingerly to the arena wall. Mom followed closely. I felt the weight of the bracelet on my wrist. I had the power to summon a monster that had done unspeakable damage, killed so many Raturro, and I felt reluctant to do so. The bracelet glinted in the sun as I rubbed it. It was our only chance for safety, so I had no choice but to use it.

Chimera, I thought. "Chimera, come," I said aloud. Mercy had said it was a tool and I had to learn to use it. But what if I failed?

The chimera exploded on the wall, shining like a million candles. The chimera was our only way out; we needed her.

"Where did you learn to do that?" Mom murmured in amazement.

"Go," I told her, and she jumped through the window of light. Next, Coyne helped Mercy through.

Alone in the arena, I glanced around one more time. I wasn't sure if I'd ever come back to Thane's Reach or if I even wanted to. It was supposed to be my home, but it didn't feel like one anymore. I turned back to the chimera and then I jumped into the light.

CHAPTER NINETEEN

The pain hit in seconds and I slumped to the ground. Everything inside of me was raw.

"We made it. We're safe," I heard Mom say through the fog in my head. We were back in the Armory. Her hand was on my back. "Kyra? Kyra?"

Coyne and Mercy ran to my side and helped me up. I looked at them all proudly. We'd made it.

"Mom!" I let her hug me with her one good arm and it felt so great to be with her again. It was worth it: all the pain and fear that I'd felt, I'd do it a hundred times over just to see her safe.

She cupped my face with her hand, crying as she kissed me on the cheek. "You are the bravest soul I know."

"And you're the Queen!" I blurted, still amazed by it all. "Why didn't you tell me?"

"Oh, Kyra, I'm just so thankful you're safe. There's so much to tell." We shared another hug, then I turned to my friends.

"You did it, Kyra. You saved us all," squeaked Mercy, and as we embraced she whispered in my ear. "You are Raturro, Ko-ru-ku."

Maybe I was after all. Coyne nodded sheepishly and shrugged. "What she said."

"*We* did it." Then we had the best group hug ever. I had two of the greatest friends I could ever hope for.

Dad rushed into the room, then stopped awkwardly when he saw Coyne and Mercy hugging me. Startled, Dad finally looked at Mom who was unrecognizable, covered in dirt and blood, but her regal force shone through. He was speechless for a moment then relief washed over him, "Aerikka, you're safe."

But Mom winced when he tried to embrace her. She held her arm protectively. "Broken, I'm sure, but Kyra has injuries that should be looked at immediately," she said and stepped back. "They all do."

Again, Dad was speechless as he took it all in. He never expected to see Mom again, that much was clear. I had dreamed of a very different reunion—loving glances, warm words between them. Though I wasn't happy to see him, I embraced Dad, but I didn't feel anything. I just knew it was the right thing to do. He brushed my hair away to examine the caked blood on my head.

"Uh, I'm okay. These are my friends, Coyne and Mercy," I said. "They helped me save Mom."

Dad grit his teeth, not happy for the reminder.

Coyne stood at attention and saluted him.

"Thank you for taking care of my daughter," Dad said, returning his salute.

"She takes care of herself pretty good," Coyne said, winking at me. "Sir," he added.

Dad's eyes went to Mercy.

"I am Merkaydees Talayna Raturro. My mother—"

"Yes. I remember you and your mother. Thank you for helping Kyra. You are both, er, welcome here," said Dad. To me he said, "We'll talk about everything that's happened once you've been treated at the clinic."

What? Was I going to get in trouble for saving Mom? I glared at him and was just about to say something I'd regret when the awkward situation was saved by a group of medics who burst into the room and rushed us all off to the infirmary.

I lay on my stomach on a gurney next to Mercy as a doctor stitched up my leg. Mercy excitedly whispered, "All of Antiica will know what you have done, Ko-ru-ku. The Raturro prophecy has come into being. You have tamed the Corvie. You have rescued the Queen. You are a hero to all."

I blushed and did kind of feel like a hero. It was a great and unexpected adventure and I was still giddy from it all. But deep down I knew that there was a bigger battle to be won.

"Mercy, I still don't understand. Why are you not on Majellan's side? Why are all the Raturro not united against the humans?"

She was deep in thought. "When my mother worked for your family, we were happy. We lived in the Cress and it was a paradise. We were young, you and I, but we never saw each other for anything more than what we were: friends. All over Antiica, there are Raturro that love humans, humans that love Raturro, and all shades of hatred that a rat could ever find. In Deep Nestling we only want peace. Majellan has become like the old Thane. There is no winner here."

Once Mercy's paw was cleaned, she revealed a single missing claw.

"Oh, Mercy, that looks so painful. It's all my fault," I said ruefully.

"I shall wear it like a badge of honour, Ko-ru-ku. There is a long and fantastic story that goes with it, after all."

Coyne joined us. He was treated for some scratches and given a fresh pair of army fatigues, which he regarded sheepishly. "Guess I'm still enlisted."

"Oh," I said, unsure. "What did my dad say?"

He shrugged and showed us the deep gouge on his arm, now stitched. Mercy scoffed at him.

"Who's the real soldier?" Mercy asked, holding up her stubby claw.

"Ouch!" he said.

I giggled, and they joined in, relieved to be alive and safe and together.

Later, I led Mercy and Coyne to Dad's quarters for a celebratory dinner.

"Are you sure I should come with you?" asked Mercy.

"Of course! Why wouldn't you?" I scoffed.

"The war is still on," she said.

"Not here," I said, dragging them both towards the room.

"This is going to be one interesting dinner," joked Coyne.

I was startled to see Varve sitting at the table. I ran to him. "Varve, you're alright!"

"Your Majesty." He jumped up to embrace me. I was so glad he was okay, but when I looked at Dad he had a sullen look on his face, as if he didn't approve of Varve.

"These are my friends, Mercy and Coyne," I said.

"I've heard a little of the story, but I'm dying to hear it all," Varve said, extending his hand to Mercy and then Coyne.

As we ate the scrumptious meal, Coyne, Mercy, and I relived our adventure all over again, each of us filling in little details: our dip in the Soulcatcher, flying high in the claws of the Corvie, and, of course, the escape from the arena. The events of our harrowing journey seemed so much easier now that they were in the past, but I wondered how Cheam and Dima were doing. I hoped they were both safe.

Mom raised her eyebrows in surprise and worry as we told our tale. Dad shook his head in disbelief, and I could tell that he was itching to pull me aside and give me a piece of his mind about running off.

I made a mental note to ask him about the two bracelets—later. I wasn't ready to bring up the Stone Wars just yet. He didn't seem surprised when I told him about the stone Majellan used to escape, but I saw him share a look of worry with Mom.

"Remarkable," was all Dad said when he reached out to squeeze my hand. We were all of us a semblance of a family that night. Human and Raturro. Like they used to do when I was little, before the war.

I still thought about the Cress, missing it even more than Earth. There was something so special about it. I felt safe there and could imagine living there again with Mom and Dad. We would sit in the sun under that old monkey puzzle tree and forget about all the strife on Antiica. Coyne and Mercy would visit, and we would swim in the lake and catch fish for dinner. Part of me knew it was a fantasy, but I needed something to look forward to, something to hold onto.

The next day, the Mess Hall was abuzz with soldiers. Mom told me that there was to be a ceremony in front of the entire Armory but she wouldn't say more. "Wait and see."

So, I was nervous when Mercy, Coyne, and I were led into the hall by Sergeant Talia. Walking proudly in her dress uniform, Talia still wouldn't make eye contact with me, and I realized she must've been blamed for me disappearing. She was supposed to watch me.

The room went quiet. On a makeshift platform at the front of the room stood Mom and Dad, very regal in their dress uniforms with an array of medals pinned to their chests. Mom was barely recognizable with her curly hair piled high on her head in a bun. She stood erect and her eyes sparkled— she even wore her scars with pride. She was a queen after all.

Coyne had been cleaned up and the new uniform made him look older, more confident. Mercy's tattered dress had been washed and repaired—she'd refused the new clothes my Mom had offered her. But her fur gleamed and she put on a brave face and held her head high in front of the soldiers. Although Mercy had cause not to, she showed a deep respect for my parents.

The worst part of the day was that Mom somehow found me a dress and had it specially altered to fit. She insisted I wear it. Uncomfortable in the scratchy blue fabric, I at least looked presentable.

I stood between Coyne and Mercy on the platform, squeezing Mercy's paw and Coyne's hand. "Nice dress, princess," he whispered sincerely as he squeezed back.

"You are witness today to great heroism," Dad addressed the crowd. "Coyne Thresh, Merkaydees Talayna Raturro, and Kyra Murch have all honoured themselves and our great country. Their brave deeds brought our queen home."

The crowd cheered while Dad stood patiently waiting for them to quiet. "I am proud of these youngsters and all they accomplished."

Dad tactfully avoided the hatred all his soldiers felt for the Raturro and made it sound like we were just kids playing a game.

Sergeant Talia brought three sashes emblazoned with the family crest—a black chimera symbol—to Dad. First he placed a sash over Mercy's shoulders then saluted her. She curtsied back. The next sash went over Coyne's shoulders and they exchanged salutes. I was last and very surprised when the crowd of soldiers clapped and cheered when I received my sash. I was proud that I'd saved Mom, but I didn't do it for them or my country. I did it because I needed my Mom. And because Dad refused to act. I still harbored anger towards him for that.

I jumped a little when Dad took my hand and led me forward, whispering in my ear, "Now you can say a few words."

I stood for a moment staring at the expectant faces in front of me. There were soldiers so young they should have been in school and grizzled men and women who would have served my father a long, long time. My eyes landed on Varve who stood at the edge of the group, but he only had eyes for Mom. Then it hit me. He was in love with Mom.

I glanced at Dad who waited a few feet away. He nodded to me—get on with it. I hadn't planned on giving a speech. All I could do was say what was in my heart.

"I know that there's been a war on Antiica for a very long time. Many of you have lost your family, your friends, but you soldier on. I've never been a fighter—never wanted to be—and I still think fighting is wrong." I heard Dad sigh.

There were rumblings in the crowd. Dad's eyes were on me, but I kept going.

"There are so many reasons to fight in this war—justice, revenge, family. I've seen terrible things. Slavery. Torture. Hatred. But most of the Raturro I've met have been kind and unbelievably brave, and I hope a peaceful solution can be found to this terrible war. We need to end the violence in our land. We need to embrace the Raturro as our friends."

The room was deathly quiet. My face burned red. Then my heart soared as Mom moved forward to stand beside me. She put her hands together and clapped. That single clap echoed through the quiet hall. Coyne and Mercy joined in. Dad had no choice but to do the same, and then all the soldiers clapped politely too.

The ceremony over, Mom embraced me; she was proud of me. "You did so well, Kyra. That wasn't so hard, was it?"

I shrugged. It kind of reminded me of my rat presentation at school. My palms were sweaty and my heart thudded in my chest. But I made it through and no one fainted.

Dad regarded me a moment. He spoke slowly, deliberately. "Your first address as a princess and you offer peace as a solution? The naïve words of a child—"

"She has spoken as she sees it," said Mom, coming to my defense. But his words stabbed me in the heart. He hadn't said it yet, but it was like he was mad at me for rescuing Mom—mad at me for even existing.

"The fresh eyes of youth should be a reminder to us that not all our answers are the right ones. The Raturro were once our friends and many have risked their lives to ensure Kyra's safety. That should not be forgotten."

Dad nodded grimly. It was a stalemate. Between us, we had our own opinions of the war, and although I knew nothing about what he'd been through I could see it was important to him. I reminded myself that I had my family back together. That was all that mattered. For now.

I was only in my quarters a moment when there was a knock at the door. Sergeant Talia darted inside my room, uninvited. Her eyes were worried, her usual confidence gone. "Princess, I must warn you," she started.

"Uh, it's Kyra," I said for the zillionth time.

"There are those who will never accept the Raturro or a truce."

"I know."

"Be careful who you trust. If you need anything. Anything. You will have my allegiance," she said. "Always." Then she slipped back out the door before I could question her.

Soon, the inevitable day came that Mercy had to return to Deep Nestling and Coyne to the Plains. I led them to the room where the chimera sat engraved on the wall. I didn't want to say goodbye, but I called the chimera and opened the portal to Deep Nestling.

Dreading to go but missing the Nestling, Mercy hugged me and thanked me for everything. "I'll visit you soon," I promised. "Oh, and tell Brae I'm sorry about losing the Rat-gah. I know it meant a lot to the Nestling."

"Yeah, me too," added Coyne.

"The Eldest Elder will understand, given the circumstances, but," she paused, troubled, "your destiny is not yet filled, Ko-ru-ku. Majellan and your father must be stopped. Peace must unite the land. It is no small task." Her eyes narrowed as she glanced at the stub where her claw used to be. The Raturro didn't forget anything easily.

I had barely given Majellan another thought since we had returned from Murch City. I felt safe in the Armory's cocoon of rock. I hoped I'd never run into him again. Ever.

"I know, Mercy. I know," was all I could say. There must be a way to end the war. There had to be.

Mercy and I hugged again. Then Coyne embraced her and I knew we would always be friends. If Coyne and Mercy can be friends, then why not others? As she walked through the chimera, Mercy glanced back, her big doe eyes brimming with tears.

"Bye, Mercy." I choked back a sob, and then she was gone. We stood for a long moment just staring into the light.

"Well…" I said. Dad had given Coyne permission to go home for the harvest, so long as he promised to return and work at the Armory. Despite knowing he would be back soon, I still felt that I was saying goodbye forever. "I wish you didn't have to go."

"Yeah. I'll be back," he said. I nodded, hoping it was true. We continued to stand there and just as I stuffed my hands in my pockets, Coyne reached out for my hand.

"Oh." I pulled my hands out and then he stuffed his hands into his pockets. Awkward. I stifled a grin.

"You, know, I couldn't have done any of this without your help."

"I know," he said with a little smirk. Our hands finally joined and I gave him an awkward kiss on the cheek that surprised us both.

"Princess." He gave a mock bow and a salute. I grinned from ear to ear. As he walked through the chimera, it was all I could do to not follow him. I reluctantly let go of his hand, and he disappeared into the brilliant light.

The chimera faded, and I was left standing alone with its sleeping outline on the wall. My head hurt a little, but I was getting used to it. Her voice in my head was louder, clearer, and it would only get better once I started my formal apprenticeship. I was not going to reject the chimera; I was going to prove to this land of Antiica that she was now a peaceful being and did not have to be feared. I would make sure of it.

I grasped my bracelet, feeling its weight on my wrist. As I leaned back against the wall, I whispered Shale's prophetic words: "Kyra of Murch, I've come to take you home."

If Antiica really was my home, I was going to stop the war and protect it—no matter the cost.

THE END

Book Two in *The Chimera's Apprentice* series arrives in Spring 2021. Get updates on *The Stone Traveller* by joining my newsletter: www.roslynmuir.com

Acknowledgements

A big thanks to my fabulous editors: Alex Yuschik and Erin Linn McMullan. A huge thanks to my beta readers: Kate Trgovac, Erika McKitrick, and Alan Pinck. And a tremendous thanks to my many readers over the years who've read some truly dreadful, early drafts: Diane Toulmin, Robert Bittner, Maggie De Vries, Linda Svendsen (UBC Thesis advisor), and Hilary McMahon.

About The Author

Scottish born Canadian, Roslyn Muir, is an award-winning screenwriter for TV and film who now believes she's a novelist. You'll often find her staring into space, always dreaming up new lands to visit (in her mind only) and monsters she can tame (well not too much). She does live with a little monster, Ripley, the Devon Rex cat. She has two fabulous, grown-up children, and one beautiful granddaughter. Once a schoolteacher, her Drama students voted her Teacher of the Year—twice! (So she must be good at something;)